WINT … REEN

by

Chris Goff

All photos/artwork by Chris Goff except:

Photo of Jack and Jill windmills (1906)
from a collection by Roy Short, reproduced with kind permission of The Jack and Jill Windmill Society

ISBN 9798564381826

https://chrisgoff8.wixsite.com

also by Chris Goff

The Land of Dreams and other stories

Dedicated to all the 'Snowflakes' out there.
For without the white of the snow,
we couldn't perceive the darkness in our midst.

Contents

Chapter One

Part the First – introducing Jack – the journey begins

All that I am about to relate to you would not have taken place without the conversation.

- *Conversation*

It started as a conversation but ended in argument.

Most arguments start over trivial matters, and this one was most trivial. I won't bore you with the minute details, the cut, thrust and parries of the argument, and how it escalated to the point of me leaving the house that dull afternoon in October.

But I want to place this as a record of how it led me to a journey of self-discovery, in this somewhat ordinary life of Jack.

It was a leaden day, one of those sludgy Sundays with no direction or pleasure. It was as if the day was pre-ordained for trouble. The rain was sporadic, the temperature not warm enough for any comfortable outdoor activity, and indoors the central heating making you feel lethargic and irritable. Too much beer and wine the night before had left a metallic taste in my mouth, and a hankering for sun and freshly squeezed orange juice – the former unlikely in the damp, dreary suburbs.

Jeanette and I had been married for 10 years and had certainly had a number of arguments before. Some culminated in one of us leaving the house for a short time, until the other capitulated and we got in to the making up process. This always happened.

Well, nearly always.

Trouble has a mind. Trouble has a way of acting like an adolescent boy in need of attention. It nags and nags until you face it head on.

There really is no need to elaborate on the content of the argument. Suffice to say it happened, and I left the house that Sunday in a woeful mood, with some intention of returning later.

This was the first week of a two-week holiday. I planned to get some decorating completed, then find time to relax. Middle age was beginning to visit me, leaving its indelible mark on my mind and body, provoking anxieties about life, work and relationships. In other words, the usual lament of men huddled in coffee shops and bars around the land.

Leaving the house that afternoon had made me revisit my insecurities, and the way that I had become comfortably soft over the past few years living with Jeanette (or *'Nettie'*, as her friends called her). How I loathed that abbreviation! It made me think of *'Last of the Summer Wine'*, and fake Constable prints hanging in themed teashops.

Climbing into the old VW camper, (not the cool split screen type, more of a *'Mystery Machine'*), I quickly realised that I had no destination.

As often happened after an argument, I could sit forlornly in a supermarket car park, licking my wounds and trying to think how I could continue to hurt Jeanette emotionally. I would watch the weekend shoppers load more than they could possibly need into overly large cars, to head off to another part of the county to gorge on yet more consumables. To my mind, they were content and happy, albeit superficially. This was an option. But not one that filled me with joy. However, before I knew it, my foot was pushing the accelerator, and the camper was moving towards the outskirts of housing estates and into retail land.

My home county is made up of three parts: coastal, countryside and town. It is also made up of three kinds of inhabitants: those who like living there, those who live there because they think they should, and those that want to get out.

I'm in the latter category.

The archetypal man in this part of the world loves beer, football and women, not necessarily in that order. I love two of those things; I love real ale and the female sex.

I have never understood the passion for football.

This may have cost me male relationships in the past, but I can do without the backslapping, cheering and insulting that accompanies the game, let alone all the man-made material that goes along with the supporter's kit.

My main passion, apart from the real ale, (although they go very nicely together), is folk music; any good traditional stuff from anywhere in the world, alongside a whole host of other genres - rock, jazz, soul.

My other passion is nature, and anything to be enjoyed in it: camping, walking, photography, birdwatching; you get the picture. This stems from childhood experiences.

But I'm getting ahead of myself. That side of the story will unfold in due course.

My audacity to suggest leaving the county was often met with derision from Jeanette. Why would you leave a place that had everything going for it! Good transport links, plentiful restaurants and entertainment, coupled with the easily accessible capital city.

For me, the delights of all this were tempered by the Thatcherite legacy of the 'if you want it you can have it' mentality.

This mindset reverberated in every part of the county, from supermarkets to road users. The egotistic triumphed. This mindset was not for me; in fact, I loathed it.

Well, that's my rant over. You get the picture. It has little to do with the unfolding story, apart from the fact that this anger, this energy that was suppressed for many of my formative years, is released, recalled in the events of the next few weeks, away from my otherwise humdrum life.

Oh, and by the way, as I previously mentioned, my name is Jack.

In my mind, and fanciful moments, I had always travelled. I fantasised about the road trips that the likes of Kerouac, another Jack, had undertaken in the 1950's and 1960's. The idea of the wild open road and its countryside filled me with longings that I thought I would fulfil 'one day'.

I had always sought the outdoors from a very early age. If I couldn't get to the woods near our house for any reason, I would immerse myself in tales of exploration from the books I borrowed regularly from the local library.

My favourites were real life tales of travelling in South America and the American West, or any good travellers' tale I could get my hands on.

I digress again…

So, with all this bubbling away in my subconscious, I went. Departed. More accurately, ran away. I left Jeanette with an earful of discontent; I left myself with a loathing and a vague notion of escape.

As I drove along the arterial roads that led away from my home - coastal, tourist plagued - I looked upon the familiar retail parks and car showrooms. They seemed to beckon the consumer, promising that the next purchase would realise their dreams, and fulfil the ache and emptiness that gnaws away in their guts.

The maudlin weather decided it wanted to be noticed, so the drops of rain that had begun to hit my windscreen became more insistent. The blades wiped away the tears that formed on the screen. It was 4 o'clock; soon dinner would be missed, and I would seek out a place to stop and lick my wounds. I felt guiltily hungry.

I should have been working out a way to repair my relationship, but my feelings of hunger prevailed, and I began to seek sustenance.

The van continued its journey, my foot stayed on the pedal, and together we conspired to motor on along familiar roads, allowing the rain to wash away our sins and guilt.

Chapter Two

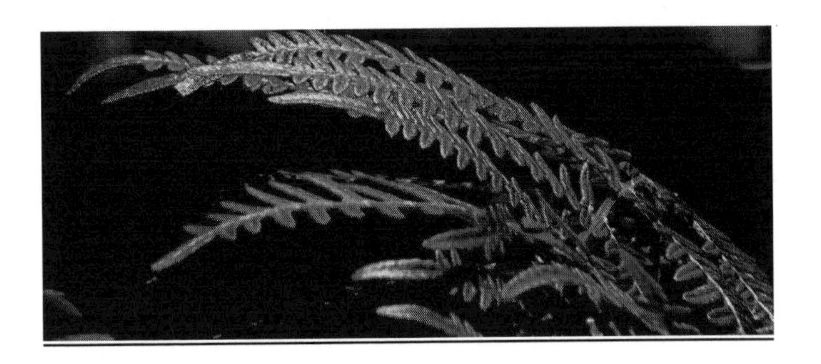

In which Jack leaves for the garden

The restaurant was familiarly unfamiliar, but it was adorned with the same tables, menu and surly service that you could get in a myriad of chain diners across the land. The food was, as usual, overloaded with fat, salt and sugar.

It was just what I needed. It was a happy meal on a sad day.

As I drove away, feeling sickeningly replete, the late Sunday sun lifted streaming bands of light along the oncoming road, as if the heavens were saying, 'come along now, let's get this thing going'.

The main arterial road led to the country's capital. I wanted to avoid that like the plague so, without too much thought, headed across the Thames towards the so-called 'Garden of England', and into the countryside.

The Garden county was initially filled with grey industrial estates, and even greyer houses. Dickens apparently spent some time in this part of England, using the gloomy, maudlin settings and grey river as inspiration for his writing. What he would make of it all now is anybody's guess. It did nothing to lift my mood, and I was keen to put the industrialisation behind me, especially on this bleak afternoon.

I wondered what Jeanette would be doing now. It was getting past the time where she may have expected a knock on the door, or a phone call with an apology. Her dinner would be eaten, mine in the bin. Calls would be made to friends, with the hope of a night on the town, where she would slag me off, and drown her troubles. I wouldn't have blamed her really. Good job we didn't have kids, to drag them in to our mess.

My thoughts were quickly replaced by practicalities, the need to find petrol and a place to park up for the night.

No campsites would be open this late in the year. I would need to find a quiet spot somewhere when I hit the countryside.

The gaudy lights of a fuel station overcame the dimming sun, and I pulled the van in to fill up alongside the lorries bound for Dover. Just thinking about these other people's journeys gave me a strange inspiration to carry on with my own, and to see where it led. After all, I had time and a credit card, so why not?

The heavy steering pulled me in to the overpriced petrol station, advertising chain coffee and cheap burgers, reminding me of my recent, badly judged, meal. The van seemed relieved to be switched off for a while, as I slid from my seat to the awaiting petrol pump.

'Some pile of junk you got there, son.'

This was spoken by a plaid shirted character who had a chromed, air horned truck on the pump adjacent to mine.

Yes,... it's quite old actually, vintage ... eighties ...'

I stuttered my reply. I didn't want to talk, I especially hated small talk anyway. I wanted to be alone with my thoughts and work out where I was heading for tonight.

'You won't make it tonight, boy. Shit, no.'

A low, phlegmy chuckle accompanied this response. He stated this with certainty, and in a mocking tone. How did he know where I was going anyway? I took a closer look at this fellow. Overweight, yet tall, he wouldn't have been out of place in a southern state hick town.

Our eyes met.

Just for a moment.

I find it difficult to recollect what happened next with any clarity.

I was back in primary school, the bell had rung for mid-morning break, and all the kids were funnelling out onto the baked tarmac of June, early 1970s. I was content to eat my handful of sweets, (chocolate raisins?), and friends seemed to have found their own way to various corners of the playground, leaving me alone amongst hundreds of children making the most of the classroom reprieve.

I was standing with my back to the blue railings that enclosed the school. I remember the pressure and heat against my bony back. I was engrossed in the white paper bag, wanting to finish the sweets before the sun and heat changed them into a sticky mess.

'How you doin', Jacky boy?'

The voice seemed to penetrate my soul. I turned slowly to see an overweight man, standing several feet away from the railings, gazing at me. He was dressed in cowboy shirt and jeans. I remember the Elvis type sideburns and huge silver signet rings on his fingers.

Things turned to sepia, and time slowed. The children's voices in the playground, once loud and intrusive, quietened, and became as muffled as the music played in the background of restaurants that we visited rarely in those days.

'Enjoying the sweetmeats?'

Sweetmeats…I had no idea what this really meant…

'We will enjoy them another time, Jacky boy.'

The man walked off down Dark Lane, the lane that I walked every day, disappearing into the sharp shadows of summer…

The sound of the nozzle being returned to the neighbouring pump brought me abruptly back to the present.

'Maybe need to get some supplies in, eh Jack?

'Long journey ahead, some sweetmeats, eh Jacky boy? Fill up that left wing, dipshit hippy belly, eh?'

The trucker was content in looking at the fuel reading on his pump. I wasn't really convinced that he had spoken aloud.

Focus!

I climbed into the van, shaking and spooked, gunned the engine and pulled away. Fuel could wait. I felt nauseous. Checking in the rear-view mirror, I could see that the truck was a huge silver beast of a thing, sign written in gothic script….

D.L.F

There was a time, when I was younger, that the thought of sleeping outdoors filled me with horror. This quickly changed after my parents went through a messy break up, my father using his bulk and strength to force a fragile relationship into submission.

I cowered in my bedroom, allowing the tinny sound of cartoons from the old TV to partially drown out rows. These were usually accompanied by the crashing of pots, pans and plates hitting woodchipped walls.

The outside seemed tranquil. The times I spent in the woods, lying on my back, gazing at the azure sky through green pines, were the happiest in my life. Strange that they transpired to become the most traumatic as well.

During that time, the woods were rarely visited by dog walkers or fitness freaks. They belonged to us. We played, set fires, shot arrows and dug for ants. I spent these idyllic times both alone, and with friends, most of whom I can barely recall.

The times alone were the most potent. The trees took on a power that was real to my young mind. In my times alone in the wood, I sometimes had the feeling of an unperceived threat, but this always passed as I became engrossed in whatever game I was playing. I remember mainly feelings of awe towards the oaks and cypress trees that became my playground, refuge and companions in childhood.

There was a spot in the woods we called, imaginatively, 'The Den'. 'The Den' had a canopy of tall oaks.

The ground had rich woodland soil, and an abundance of ferns. There was an indentation in the ground, and this made for a perfect place to rest after playing 'war', or just being together on the long, hot summer days of the school holidays…

As the van trundled down the motorway, my thoughts about childhood were interrupted by the need to find a spot to park and make camp for the evening. I still needed fuel. The gauge was creeping towards red.

The remaining light of the dull day was almost gone, drivers were heading home to family and cosy nights in front of the TV. I wasn't too sure where I was heading, but already it felt like I was on a rollercoaster that I couldn't get off, an unplanned ride but nevertheless exciting.

The next exit I saw pulled me towards it, and I soon found that I was heading into the more verdant countryside of Kent, albeit shrouded in the diminishing light. I was leaving the racetrack to the Channel behind.

A small hamlet, which to this day I can't place on any map, came into view. It had the obligatory church, oak beamed pub with swinging sign and, of course, the village green.

On my left, a small side road headed up towards what looked like woodland. I drove up as far away from any houses as possible, turned off the engine and took stock of my day.

The lane was quiet and secluded, just what I was looking for. Nobody to disturb me or worry that I was going to taint their neighbourhood with left wing hippy ideals…

'(...a camper! Must be a dipshit leftie hippy, Jacky boy!)'

So here I was, in an unknown village, wife at home, (or maybe clubbing?), and the evening to kill. I felt spent. The incident at the petrol station had unsettled me, and the smell of busy roads and fast food had left me faintly nauseous. Alcohol and undemanding strangers were needed, and the pub seemed a good enough choice to start my venture.

I began my walk down the unlit road towards the village pub. An owl hooted in a tree not far away.

The traffic noise of the major road I had recently left could be heard faintly, the now clear evening allowing sound to travel easily.

The hum of a truck moving up through its gears made me pick up my pace and head for light, warmth and human company.

Chapter Three

In which Jack makes an acquaintance, meets tribulation, and finds some answers

The *'Lynch'* public house revealed itself after a while. Few lights shone from the window, but the aroma of stale cooking oil preceded its appearance and led me to the doorway.

I had envisaged the typical horror film entrance - walk in, conversation ceases, walk to the bar, order the local brew from the landlord, (unhospitable), locals whispering something vaguely sinister under their breath.

I was welcomed, however, by a yellow three-legged dog, and a smile from the pierced and tattooed barmaid.

'What do you recommend?', I asked, as I took in the Siouxsie Sioux vest top.

'We have some local ales on tap. The natives tend to drink the lager.'

In an effort to be inconspicuous, I ordered a pint of lager. I watched the glass being filled and puzzled on the strange comment made earlier by the trucker. Contrary to his belief I had made it, albeit only to the local pub, but it was a start. Also, I had a cosy spot to rest up for the night, until I decided my plans for the following day. The barmaid placed the pint on the beermat and held out a hennaed hand for my money.

The *'Lynch'* had few redeeming features; anaglypta wallpaper from the 1980s, and a few scattered pictures on the wall, mainly pastoral scenes. Tables and chairs that had seen wear and better days, again probably from the same era. As I sat with my pint, I gazed at a picture hanging in an alcove opposite. Something about the faded print of the countryside and its characters drew me in.

There was a farmer and his farmhands lifting bales of hay onto a wagon pulled by horses; an old lady sat on a cottage step teasing a ball of wool.

A young woman, who was very pretty, sat with her back against an oak tree, gazing outwardly from the canvas, Mona Lisa style. In the distance an immense forest was evident. The girl wore a green dress, which was spread across the dusty ground. She had bright coppery coloured hair and intense green eyes.

'She's beautiful, isn't she?'

The barmaid was next to me, mopping up the previous customer's beer from my table.

'Yes', I replied, 'reminds me of a girl I used to know.'

'She hasn't been here for a while', the girl said.

'What do you mean?', I asked, confused, 'the painting has just gone up?'

'No…er...never mind. Are you having another?'

I had already drunk the beer, drawn in by the picture on the wall. Time had passed very quickly; I had been looking at the picture, and the girl in it, for nearly an hour according to the clock on the wall.

'I'd better get going, busy day tomorrow. Thanks for the welcome...er…'

'Ami', she said, 'my name's Ami. See you around.'

As I trudged up the cold, dark lane my thoughts went to the girl in the picture. She was so familiar it left me feeling unsettled and annoyed that I couldn't place her. In the near distance, a truck lumbered on the country lanes, a blast from an air horn announcing its presence. I shivered.

The van looked lonely in its isolated spot, but welcoming. The thought of a well-deserved rest was appealing, and I was pleased that I had pulled out the bed before going to the pub. I unlocked the sliding door and climbed in, keeping the light off to avoid unnecessary attention. I undressed and threw my clothes onto the front seat.

Sliding into the sleeping bag and putting my head down, I was irritated to find that I had left something on the pillow. Turning on the interior light revealed a small white paper bag, along with a handwritten note in gothic script.

You made it this far, Jacky boy!
Enjoy the sweetmeats, your
favourites if I remember rightly.

For a moment I stared at the words, not really comprehending what they meant. I opened the bag. It was filled with small chocolate balls. I guessed - chocolate raisins.

The adrenaline kicked in, as my mind flew over different scenarios. How far away was my unwelcome guest?

Hastily, I packed the bed away, dressed and climbed into the driver's seat. I gunned the engine, turned the van around in a messy three-point turn, and sped back down the lane. I had no destination but needed bright lights to put this nightmare into perspective. Turning right at the end of the lane, I picked up speed along the country road I had driven on only a few hours before.

In the distance, a lonely figure was walking ahead of me. My headlights picked up bright orange hair and a slim figure, clad in a camouflaged army jacket. Ami from the *'Lynch'!*

Normally I wouldn't have pulled over for a woman on a dark night, but this evening was anything but normal. I felt reassured to see a familiar face after my shock. I reached over and wound down the window.

'Can I give you a lift?'

Ami looked at me with concerned eyes, then with a cry said, 'Jack! Thank God it's you!

'I was worried. After you left, strangers came into the pub, asking about you. You need to go! Go somewhere safe, you can't be seen out here! Go home. Now!'

I hadn't recalled telling Ami my name, but she was too het up for me to pursue this while she was standing in the lane. Tonight was getting weirder by the hour.

'We need to talk, Ami. I'm confused, and I need to know what the hell is going on! And how do you know my name?'

Ami clambered into the van, bringing with her the scent of stale beer, rollups and patchouli. It was a smell that reminded me of times past and brought some reassurance and reality back to an abnormal night. She sighed, stretched, and got out her tobacco pouch (well-worn polished leather, very much like one I had owned in my youth).

'Do you mind?'

'No, go ahead' I said, 'I used to, but gave up. Too many regulations around now to make it enjoyable. Plus, they stopped my blend.'

'Where do you want me to start, Jack?'

'Start by telling me what you know about me', I said.

'Okay, here goes. You may not believe all I say, and that's up to you, but you need to know some of the fundamentals otherwise I'm not doing my job properly and you are very unsafe at the moment.'

'What do you mean...job?'

'Stay with me here Jack, it may become clearer. You recognised the girl in the picture, didn't you? She is someone you used to know, someone you used to know very well in fact. You do remember your childhood sweetheart, don't you, Jack?'

I did. Of course I did.

Back to the den every day in summertime, this was our refuge from warring families and the adult world we didn't understand.

Jenny was one of the boys really. We were 11; we didn't understand or care about the complexities of gender.

We ran, we fought, and we played. That was it. No agenda, 'just be' day to day.

These days we strive to 'just be' by attending mindfulness courses, Yoga or such like…then, well it was simple, day to day, hour by hour. Play all day, get tired, go home, sleep, and start again the next day.

Days seemed to last forever. No school bells to instruct timetabled days. Just do what comes naturally.

Jenny. When did the attraction begin? I guess sometime between throwing mud clumps at each other, and beginning to tell each other about our deepest fears, or hopes, for the future. There was no formal 'asking out' or date. We were just comfortable in each other's presence on those long, hot summer days.

We played war, we played hide and seek, and we built fires in the den. Jenny wore a pair of denim dungarees and the yellow baseball cap her aunt brought back from America…the cap she treasured, and it never left her head, tousled ginger locks spilling from the back of it.

The day she went missing was the day that my life stopped.

The yellow cap.

That was the only thing they found the next day, hung on the oak we had swung on the previous afternoon, a few orange hairs caught in the rear bronze clasp…

Then, all at once I became aware of adultness, and the harsh adult world. The bubble that we had created in our childish world, suddenly burst. I can't remember playing as a child played, from that day onward.

Memories, of course, came flooding back. The days and weeks that followed Jenny's disappearance were limbo days. As I sat, often alone now, in the Den, I would wait, hoping that I would hear her call my name as she sauntered into the wood. But as the weeks turned into months and the summer inevitably gave way to colder days, the hope gradually diminished.

No body was ever found. Several local men were arrested and questioned about the case, men that were known to the community as 'odd', but no charges were ever made. Difficult when you don't have a body.

That day's events had plagued me ever since. Could we have done anything to save Jenny? We left her that afternoon, alone, in the den, putting out the fire.

'Go', she said. She insisted it's what she liked to do.

'I like to see a fire dead', she said, 'otherwise I worry and can't sleep.'

The fire was still smouldering the following day when the police asked us to take them to the den. Jenny had been taken, or worse, extinguished, unlike the fire she left last evening.

'Let's go, Jack. I can tell as much as I know but sitting here on the side of the road is risky. I need a drink and a sit down. That pub does my bloody head in.'

Ami directed me down long country lanes and, although it was dark, I could see the woodland on either side of the road was dense and ancient.

'Stop here.'

She awoke me from my reverie, and I pulled over into a dirt layby on the edge of a tree lined lane.

'We walk from here, Jack. My place is 20 minutes away - can you make it?'

She laughed as she said this, blowing out a long stream of sweet tobacco smoke, a smell that made me crave a roll up after so many years.

I followed Ami as best I could, deeper into the woodland. She used no light and was as nimble as a ballet dancer as she navigated fallen branches and roots in the darkness that enveloped us. The smell of the woods, mixed with tobacco, was heady; the cold air made our breath leave misty trails in our wake.

I stumbled along with her, following a girl I barely knew, deep into woodland I didn't know at all. This was madness; the day was madness…

'Here we are', she said, and a small wooden door appeared as if by magic in front of us.

'This is my home; welcome to *'Green'*.'

Chapter Four

A new shoot comes from a fallen tree

We sat in a small room, constructed and furnished completely out of wood, some of it living. Candlelight cast its flickers all around, showing the room had no corners. It appeared to be formed out of the woodland itself.

Ami sat in a chair fashioned, as far as I could see in the subdued light, of curved and twisted wood, giving the impression that she was supported by roots. She motioned me to sit on a couch, covered in what I thought was green velvet. It was immediately comfortable, and I could feel the tiredness and stresses of the day leaching from me.

We drank ale which, according to Ami, was far superior to the muck in the *'Lynch'*. I couldn't disagree. The beer had a sensuous, hoppy taste that I hadn't experienced for many years.

'Where is this from?', I asked.

'Look around, Jack!'

As I did, the dimly lit room began to reveal wooden barrels, supported on trusses to allow the tapping of the beer. There must have been at least fifteen barrels as far as I could see in the gloom.

'You brew your own, then?'

'Yes, but I get help', she replied. 'It can be an onerous task collecting the hops and starting the fermentation process…worth it though, eh?'

Ami rolled another cigarette. She saw my longing look, and when she had deftly made her own, threw the pouch to me.

'I don't think my wife would be happy. You are getting me started on bad habits again, Ami!'

I was gratified that I remembered how to roll a cigarette after years of abstinence; like riding a pushbike, you never quite forget how.

I remembered the times in my teenage years, sitting out late with friends as we discussed the meaning of life, smoking homemade cigarettes, sour bellies filled with too much ale. The process of making a cigarette, pinching the right amount of tobacco from your favourite tin or pouch, was an integral part of those times.

Ami's yellow tobacco smelt of vanilla. I rolled my first cigarette in years.

'You will leave here with more questions than you came with', Ami said, taking a swig of beer, followed by a long draw on her roll up. 'There is so much you don't know about what is happening Jack, but I know a bit more than most, so here goes.'

Ami settled herself into the woodland seat, which looked like it had moulded itself around her.

'You may think that all that has happened today is strange. Well it is, but you have opened portals that have been closed for many years. Leaving your home sent a warning to those who thought you were safely cocooned in domesticity.

'They were watching you, and now you are dangerous to 'them'.'

‘I’m not sure I quite understand’, I replied.

‘How am I dangerous, and who are ‘them’?’

I was experiencing a pleasant feeling from the sweet tobacco, and was beginning to feel sleepy, but I was enthralled by Ami’s story.

‘This may be hard to hear, Jack. You remember this evening I told you to go back home?’

‘Yes, of course’, I replied. ‘I wondered then how you knew I had left my wife?’

‘Well’, Ami began, ‘am I wrong in saying that you and your wife have never been that connected? Sorry if that sounds forward, but time is short, and we need to speak with honesty.’

‘Bloody hell Ami, you can speak honestly but I have only known you a few hours! What gives you the right to make that sort of judgement, and how would you know that anyway?’

‘I told you this would be hard, Jack. You can think what you like of me, but you need to hear what I have to say.’

I looked at her.

She was quite ethereal in her chair of the woodland, her bright orange hair framing an elven like face. She had a wisdom and serenity about her that I had only seen occasionally.

'Please, carry on', I said.

I took a draught from the glass of ale that was now only half full.

'I said tonight that you needed to go back to her. That was a bit of a test. You need to understand that you were both, well, engineered to be together. Unknown to you then, others working for 'him' sought to distract you away from the future that you were called for.'

Ami continued, 'You know Jack, I met Jeanette a long time ago. She was nice, but we didn't really hit it off. If you allow yourself to deal with the anguish, you know who your only love is.'

'Is?', I said. Ami made no comment and inhaled deeply on her cigarette.

'If it wasn't for the fact that you seem really nice, and you're giving me sanctuary from whatever is out there, I would go. Ami, thank you for your help tonight but you are crossing a line here with this personal stuff.'

As I spoke, I could only wonder at Ami, and the strange surroundings I had entered. The statement that she had made about my only love had hit me like a hammer, forcing me to feel things I hadn't felt for many years. I was glad of the poor light as I felt a tear run down my cheek. I took a long draw on my roll up, the glowing tip briefly lighting the small room.

'People talk about conspiracy theories', Ami continued, 'most are rubbish of course, and there is no reason to suppose otherwise. Our people are fighting bigger issues than all the terrorists and corrupt politicians put together.

'The signs are not hidden on the dollar bill or found in Masonic lodges, but in the rivers and woodlands, mountains and valleys. Most people don't pay too much attention to the environment that surrounds them. Take a walk in a forest with someone who says they 'just love nature'! See if they are as attuned to the sights, sounds and movements as we are, Jack.'

Ami was right. So many times, I had taken walks with people through the most beautiful countryside, and they had filled the precious time with inane talk and blundering footfall, the creatures I had spotted quickly retreating from us, as they sought refuge from their constant foe.

'Over the years, Jack, populations of all species around the world have decreased. Birds, insects, reptiles, mammals; all have declined over the years due to irresponsible farming, industrialisation, greed and pollution. Jack, you need to understand what part you are destined to play to help stop all this. This may surprise you, but I assure you it's true.

'You see, Jenny was a threat to those that wanted to continue to destroy and corrupt the earth for their own gain. Jenny, even at 11, knew this. She was wise, far beyond her years. She was taken to prevent her from becoming one with you…that could never be allowed, there was too much at stake for them. That shows how potent you are, Jack. But both of you together would have been a disaster for their plans.'

Jenny was gone, I thought, but it seemed she had not been forgotten. She still had influence…

'You married a nice, but incompatible, companion. This arrangement perfectly suited their needs - until now. Now they are worried that you are not as docile as they thought. Worried you will interrupt their plans. Very worried.'

I sat for a while thinking on Ami's words. I needed to leave. It was obvious she lived in a fantasy world, no doubt fed by strong ale and a vivid imagination.

'You probably think I'm mad', she stated, obviously reading my expression.

'Well, it's not your average story, is it?', I said. 'I am curious to know how you found out so much about me!' Before I could continue, she began talking again.

'I said there would be more questions than answers. Stay the night. You can sleep in here; you will be safe. I'll get things ready for you. Finish up your ale, Jack, tomorrow may be interesting! We can talk more in the morning.

'There is something you need to know though. Although Jenny was never found, it doesn't mean she is gone forever. I won't say too much tonight; it's been a long and exhausting day for you. The woman in the picture hanging in the pub, she had an effect on you didn't she, Jack?'

Jenny.

Jenny. Taken but still living with me in my memory.

Who was I kidding? I still loved her.

But of course, how dumb of me! The woman in the picture, she looked like Jenny, or how Jenny would have looked if she had been allowed to grow up.

But there were so many unanswered questions. Feelings of rage and longing filled me, the tear that I had shed earlier began to form again. I was unsure whether to explode with anger towards Ami's insensitivity, or cry with the hope that the girl I had once loved was still alive.

Ami said, 'You're tired, Jack. Take this blanket, make yourself comfortable on the floor and dream peacefully.'

Ami grabbed a blanket from a hook above her head and passed it to me. It felt wonderfully soft, was featherlight, and had the smell of woodland and woodsmoke that was so evocative to me of years past. The ale and weariness were fogging my mind. I looked around the dim room to find a place to rest.

'You will find the floor remarkably soft and comforting, Jack.'

With that, Ami leant towards me and kissed my temple maternally, then without another word slipped from the room, leaving behind her heady scent of tobacco, patchouli and beer.

I pulled the blanket over me and lay down on the ground.

There was no carpet or floorcovering. The unevenness of the earth made me question Ami's statement about comfort. Incredibly, when I stretched my tired body out, it was as though the very woodland itself was embracing me; bumps on the ground moulded themselves exquisitely into the contours of my body. I was to spend my first night at *'Green'*.

I rested my head onto what seemed like moss; the strong aroma of the woodland surrounded me, and the drowsiness that I had felt earlier quickly rushed over me. As my body began to enter sleep, it felt that the earth and I had entered a relationship. I believed I could understand the silent communication of the woodland as the creatures and trees embraced the approaching night.

Sleep.

Dreams.

Ants, millipedes, caterpillars, all had their language, differing, but common to the woodland itself. Even the trees were communicating with each other; they were sonorous and commanding, compared to the tiny creatures babbling below my head.

The chattering of the woodland was more beautiful and vibrant than any symphony created by man.

With my eyes shut, I could still envisage the image of the chair Ami had just vacated, and the line of beer barrels that encircled the room. Very quickly it seemed, I fell into sleep, the beer making me soporific, and more than ready for…

Sleep.

Dreams.

In my dream, I saw again the beer barrels that encircled the room; I saw the oak trees that each of them was made from. Then, in my dream, I heard the trees, as I heard the other creatures in the wood, only they had more authority…

'We are the oak, Jack; we are the ancient, and soon we will be no longer. 10,000 years before your Christ God, we were on the earth. We thrived, along with our brothers and sisters: Willow, Hazel, Elm, Yew and Pine.

'In the first 100 years after the Christ God, half of us had been felled for fire to warm humans, and fuel forges to shape metal from the ground.

'We were cut, chopped and burned without thought or mercy, and we wept with the sap that is our lifeblood.

'We have been harvested throughout your history for man's use and greed. We were used to make instruments of torture and death. We were cut down, then resurrected to hang your Christ God from. We were used for ships to carry mortal cargo across the oceans, the blood and excrement from your kind soiling and soaking into our grain.

'Later, we looked to those that could see our desperate plight. Some of you formed assemblies because they could see the danger the earth was in; some also sailed the oceans trying to stop the slaughter of the creatures that live there. They also went to forests to stop the cutting and felling of our kind.

'Most of you ignored us.

'But Jack, a new shoot comes from a fallen tree…"

Then in my dream I was back to my 11th year.

I was sitting on the gaudy Axminster carpet in my parent's living room; the new colour television with its three channels was showing 'Merrie Melodies', my favourite cartoon show.

It was strange watching myself; I looked small and vulnerable but happy to be in 'cartoon land'.

The programme changed; a topical children's news programme came on. I remember I would ordinarily turn the television off at this point ('waste all the electricity you want, Jacky boy!').

In my dream, I could see all the rooms in the house. Mum and Dad were arguing in the kitchen again, so television seemed a good way to distract myself from the pain I felt listening to them attack one another…

'The environmental group Greenpeace are in Greenland, spraying baby seals in dayglo to mark their pelts, making them valueless to the hunters who club them to death. There are images in the next clip some viewers may find disturbing.'

The VT runs: a Greenpeace activist is shown squaring up to a hunter, grisly club in his bloodstained hand. A baby seal looks up at them with big brown liquid eyes, the activist reaches into the pocket of their parka coat and manages to discharge some spray on to the seal. As the camera pans on to the activist, we see a head swathed in hood and balaclava, and briefly see a stray lock of red hair escaping from the hood, blowing in the cold Arctic air…

…a logger deep in the Amazon rainforest is caught on camera by a Greenpeace activist.

With chainsaw in hand, and huge truck to transport the felled trees, the logger grins toothlessly at the camera. The activist continues to film the logger, whose smile is now turning into something more sinister. Heckled by a bunch of leathery men, who begin to shout abuse and profanities, the red-haired girl continues filming, as they try to wrestle the camera from her…

'Wake up, Jack!'

Ami's face slowly came into view as my eyes opened, and I surfaced from the visions I had seen during the night.

'Are you OK, Jack? You have been making some very strange sounds!'

Two sunbeams lit the small room from the windows behind me. In the early morning, just enough daylight illuminated the room that I had slept in to see more clearly than I had the previous evening.

The barrels of beer took on a new look for me as I recalled my dream, just moments before. The oak that they were made from seemed as if it were alive. Indeed, knots in the barrel facing me seemed as though they were two eyes, watching me as I had slept.

As my eyes adjusted, I looked at my sleeping area, and was not entirely surprised to see that I had slept on deep pile green moss, growing between two enfolding tree roots. Like my grandfather's briar pipe, these fat roots were buffed to a smooth, silky finish by former inhabitants.

'I'm OK. Strange dreams though!'

Ami was standing with two steaming mugs in her hands, from the aroma filled with freshly brewed coffee - that wonderful smell which always managed to arouse my slumbering mind and body. Backlit in the early morning sunlight, Ami's red hair shimmered, looking delightfully unearthly.

'A mug of coffee before you go on your way? Cigarette?'

'No thanks, I don't really want to start again.'

Who was I fooling, of course I did!

'Tell me more about this place though.'

'This place is very special, Jack. It has been created and moulded by the woodland over many, many years. It has been given to men by the earth as a very precious gift. I am very honoured to be part of a long line of its temporary caretakers. I hope you will remember your stay in here. Very few have experienced the likes of '*Green*'.'

'It all sounds very wistful Ami, but what do you mean, "moulded by the woodland"?'

'Well, an age ago there were dwellings like this all over the world.

'They were hidden by Mother Nature; she created these havens because the natural world was beginning to be destroyed by one of its most deadly and destructive inhabitants. Humankind.

'These special places became known only to a chosen few, the few that cared for more than just draining the earth for its minerals and whatever else it would give up. Places like *'Green'* were there to help keep a check on what damage man was wreaking on the planet. From England to Australia, these small oases were in constant undetectable communication with each other, conversing in a language that was ancient and clear, communicating of the inevitable, creeping enemy. Unfortunately, one by one they have been found and destroyed so that only a handful survive. This place is one of the remaining few.

'Green' is only a couple of miles from a main road on which thousands pass each day, but so far it has remained undiscovered. Walkers pass by regularly, but they are blind to this place. The woodland keeps it so.'

I must have looked bewildered as Ami continued.

'You see, Jack, you being here is no accident! The connection you had with woodland as a boy led you here today. It has been intended, ordained if you like. In fact, from the day you last saw Jenny, this day was written in your destiny.'

Every time I heard her name a sharp pain went through me. It had been 30 years since I last saw her, but I remember her voice as clearly as if it were yesterday…

'Go! Go home, Jack! Your dad will be mad if you stay out any later. I will put this fire out, then I'll go home.'

She smiled at me then, the sort of smile that is branded on your memory, like when you glance at the sun and it burns the back of your eyes, and you still see its shape with your eyes closed for a few moments. The image like an old sepia photograph.

'The biggest problem in the world today', Ami continued, 'is the issue of overpopulation of our planet. We build and build using more materials and clearing more land; the Earth simply cannot replenish itself quickly enough. In other words, Jack, we are running out of time. Nature is very forgiving; it has always bounced back, but it is telling us now that this cannot go on. Unless we wake up, the planet we live on will die…and we will be gone for ever.

'I can't give you any explanations, Jack, but I know, and you may be beginning to see, that you, along with others, have been chosen to stop the futile road we are taking. Unfortunately, you have some powerful adversaries, and they know you are abroad.'

For a brief moment I wanted to ring Jeanette, apologise, get into the van and drive home; I could be home in just over an hour, but Ami interrupted my thoughts.

'Why don't you call Jeanette, Jack, tell her you will be away for a while, smooth things over with her and then I can tell you what I think you need to do, if you'll let me?'

Chapter Five

Oh, what a circus!

I recalled the day that I made my way home from school many years ago. Jenny and I had talked about it frequently, tried to make sense of it, until her disappearance.

The sharp autumn air made the children walk briskly from school that day. I walked along Dark Lane, the bare trees creating a cathedral like canopy above, filtering out any light, even on sunny days.

The children's voices became fainter the further I walked away from the school. Other children who walked this lane thinned out as they took side paths to their homes, towards television and tea.

My mind wandered over the school day. As usual it had been filled with fear and trembling. Most of the teachers took great delight in making us scared, especially one teacher - my tutor, Mr. Finch. (Elderly, balding, always immaculately dressed, with a substantial corporation that was usually covered in a waistcoat - you never forget this stuff). It would be years before I learned the words 'sadist' and 'paedophile'. This man was surely both.

I would be thankful to get home to the warmth and cartoons that would be on TV; I hoped that my parents were not arguing already.

The light was fading fast this autumn afternoon. I quickened my pace and refused to think about the dark rumours that the children in school had whispered about the lane.

Walking briskly now, I distracted myself by thinking about the recent episode of 'Timeslip', the story of two kids finding companionship and adventure when they stumbled into a Ministry of Defence compound which took them spiralling backwards in time.

To my right, along the line of the ditch, a flash of white caught my eye, and soon afterwards a boisterous fluttering sound.

Nervously, I looked sideways.

Caught in the tangle of branches at the bottom of the ditch was a bird.

Gingerly, I stepped off the muddy path and looked down. At first, I saw only the bird, then I saw the hand.

The bird was being held by the man who days earlier had talked to me through the school railings.

He was crouched in the mud, and partially hidden by the branches and undergrowth. The bird - I think it was a dove, pure white and beautiful - looked at me with clear, dark jewelled eyes. The man caressed the creature, almost lovingly, in his cupped hands.

I was mesmerised, and it was difficult to remove my gaze from its hopeless, terrified eyes.

A sound began to issue from the man's throat, nearly like laughter, along with a ghastly screeching sound. The bird began struggling; its pleading eyes met mine, and slowly but surely, as the man's laughter became stronger, the light from the eyes of the bird dimmed and then was extinguished.

The life of this creature was leisurely and purposefully squeezed out of it.

Silver ringed fingers relaxed and dropped the bird to the ground, accompanied by a throaty sound of delight…

Of course, I was too young to grasp the full meaning of this act. In retrospect I can now see the cruel imagery. The symbol of peace. Destroyed.

Ami stretched back in her seat. 'It's time to show you some of '*Green*'.

'You can call your wife when you get outside; I'm afraid there is no signal in here. I want to show you something first though.'

Ami stood, and with surprising strength, pulled me up from my 'bed' on the ground. With a sparkle in her eyes, she beckoned me to the other side of the room.

I hadn't noticed any other door except the one I had come through directly from the woodland but, pulling back a heavy jade coloured curtain from along the wall, she revealed a small wooden door shaped much like the beer barrels in the room. As we crouched and passed through the door, an overwhelming aroma of fresh forest pine drifted up from the floor.

Pine fronds were carefully arranged on the ground, so every step released the fresh perfume.

The 'room' was much larger than the one we had come from. There were no windows, but candles were all around, set on shelves and cupboards, all seemingly made from forest materials.

'This place has been here many years, Jack. I was lucky enough to be introduced to it by my predecessor who lived here about 5 years ago.

'I was much like you are now, struggling with modern life and its indifference to the damage it was wreaking on the planet. I was also in a difficult and tiresome relationship. When I was brought here, I slept in the same room you did last night, and probably had similar dreams and visions.'

She looked at me as if waiting for some response, but I could give none. Once again, my senses were overwhelmed.

'Mankind has historically communicated with their gods through prayer. We commune with the natural world through stewardship and close contact. Like other faiths, we are sometimes guided by dreams and visions. We stay in close contact with Mother Earth through places like *'Green'*.

'This place is special because the contact is pure and ancient. We are in tune with nature here as nowhere else. The oak roots you slept in the middle of last night are very special because of their age and wisdom.'

'How old?', I asked.

‘I’m not sure. There are many things I still don’t understand, but the oak spoke to me through my dreams of their relationship with the ancient peoples who were living in these woods many eons ago. They spoke in a very different tongue than we do; they also had a greater understanding of the relationship between nature and mankind which we have now tragically lost.

‘The ancient Celts considered the oak as a storehouse of wisdom embodied within its towering strength. The immense growth, imposing spread and longevity led them to believe that it was a symbol to be revered, both for its endurance, and its noble existence. We do the same, Jack. Unfortunately, much of society now regards the old ways as redundant, and mocks believers as misguided environmentalists, or, at worst, dismisses them as hippies or tree huggers.

‘It has become clear to me, Jack, that you are here to help with combatting influences that wish to damage the earth.’

I had always felt deeply that I needed to do more for the environment, and something in what she said made sense. My thoughts swung between total acceptance of Ami’s conclusion or…she was insane. I needed some air.

'This has all been great, Ami', I said, 'but I really need to be getting on now. I am really thankful for your help, and for letting me stay in this enchanted lodging for the night, but I am on a sort of holiday. I need the sea and a few days to sort out my head with my relationship problems.'

'As you please, Jack. You know that I will be at the *'Lynch'* if you want to meet again.'

'Thanks Ami…I won't forget this in a hurry, thanks again it's been…ah, you've been great.'

We hugged awkwardly, as I made my way to get my things together.

We walked back through the curtain, the room I had slept in the previous night, and once again through the small wooden door, out into the grey, early morning light of the woodland, with the mist hanging in the branches. It could have been my overly attuned sensitivity, but as we walked from *'Green'* I swore I saw fleeting glimpses of animals retreating into the greyed woodland, followed by muffled snaps of fallen twigs as they hid from sight.

'They wanted to hear your answer', Ami stated, as if reading my thoughts.

Ami led the way we had trodden only a few hours earlier, back to my camper. To my relief, the van was still there.

The sweet wrapper incident was an aberration; did it really happen?

I was still keen to return to some sort of urbanisation and normality, although the woodland experience had touched me very deeply.

The windows of the van were misted, the van itself covered in early morning dew and cobwebs. Bizarrely, under the wipers on the windscreen, someone had put a gaudy paper flier, the sort left in town car parks.

I snatched the flier from the screen, expecting offers of cheap pizza or burger meals.

Instead, I found a lurid picture of a woman, red hair cascading down her bare back, her arms raised, whip in one hand and an elephant staring, entreatingly, into her eyes…

D.L ENTERTAINMENTS PRESENTS:

CIRCUS!

ROLL UP! ROLL UP!

CIRCUS! CIRCUS!

COME AND SEE!

THE GREATEST SHOW ON EARTH!

(WHILE IT LASTS)!

BEARS! LIONS! TIGERS!

AND OUR ENCHANTING WILD BEAST TAMER

MISS JENNI!

I pulled the misted van door open.

Inside.

Filled.

Flyers.

Flyers stacked from roof to floor. Glossy and thick. Not an inch of space; the artificial smell of fresh print filled my nostrils.

I was gripped by nausea as I pulled a random flyer from the stacks.

CIRCUS!

ROLL UP! ROLL UP!

Sickness overcame me and, as I threw up down the side of the van, I could taste the print chemicals and, bizarrely, chocolate.

I was aware of Ami in my peripheral vision. Crying.

Looking at the earth, my sickness leaking into it, I noticed that my tires had been let down. Not slashed but deflated. I couldn't leave just yet even if I wanted to.

'Jack', Ami was talking through sobs, 'I'm sorry this has happened. Can you understand how real this is now?'

Ami's tears had left black mascara lines down her cheeks as she sobbed and spoke.

Regaining composure, she said, 'I will get Harry at the pub to sort the tyres out but first I have something for you.'

She reached down and picked up a rucksack. I hadn't noticed that she had been carrying anything before.

'I've had this prepared for a while now Jack, it was sitting, waiting in *'Green'*. I believe it has found its rightful owner. Please, take it with you.'

'Take it with me? I'm not sure I understand!'

'You need to go on your journey, Jack...to find yourself and recognize your calling. Get back in touch with that urge to explore that you have suppressed for so long. Isn't it clear now that the time is right for you to go? You can't stay here any longer, it's too dangerous.'

I considered my options. Either I try to get the van sorted and drive off, or go against my nature and be impulsive, take the rucksack, and have an adventure. Ami had struck a nerve. She was spot on with my inner feelings about taking risks.

'Where do you suggest I go, Ami?'

"It's all down to you, Jack, but I have a map of a route that was taken many years ago, by a wayfarer, long before we were born. It leads to another sanctuary like *'Green'* which is in Sussex, on the Downs.

'It may be an idea to start there. Be instinctual though, go with your spirit and nature will look out for you, I'm sure.'

I wasn't too convinced by what Ami was saying, but the sense of excitement that I had quelled so many times in the past came bubbling to the surface. If I didn't take this opportunity now, when would I? When I was too old, too scared, or too wrapped up with possessions and more commitments? I reached for the rucksack which felt surprisingly light for such a journey.

'It's all there, Jack, all you will need for your undertaking. Tread lightly and gently. I will look forward to seeing you soon to hear all about it. Give me the keys to your van; I will make sure it's kept safe.'

'Thanks, Ami. Can I contact you in any way, you know, if things get weird?'

'I'll be here at *'Green'* or working at the '*Lynch*'; you can call me there during pub hours. I don't do mobiles, not much point in *'Green'*, no reception. Take care, Jack; I think you should get moving. Staying here too long is not a good idea. Your trucker friend is not too far away, I believe.'

With that disquieting announcement Ami left, melting into the woodland, leaving me with the clothes I stood in, and a rucksack with dubious, and by the sounds of it, interesting contents.

Chapter Six

The long walk

'I'm sorry, the person you have called is not available right now; please leave a message and they will get back to you.'

'Jeanette, it's me....I....I just wanted to let you know I'm OK....I'm in Kent, I've had a bit of an adventure...I will probably stay away for a few nights...we need to talk...call me.'

Shouldering the old rucksack, (surprisingly comfortable), and standing on the threshold of goodness knows what, felt simultaneously exhilarating and forbidding.

To my right stood a deflated van, to my left somewhere in the woods an enchanted dwelling, and directly in front of me the unknown Replacing my dying mobile in my army jacket pocket, I began walking to the south, hopefully in the direction of the Sussex Downs.

As good a plan as any, I thought.

The woodland issued the calls of crows living in the high treetops, their lofty nests silhouetted in the pale sky. Stipples of sunlight broke through the trees, illuminating the fallen autumn leaves. Foliage was scarce this time of the year, so birds were glimpsed in the morning light, as the early mist faded. The faint sound of a truck changing up through its gears overcame the birdsong; it awoke a foreboding in me and prompted me to begin walking.

Swiftly.

The woodland was dank and gave out the smell of dead vegetation that I remembered from my childhood.

The path at this point was clear and easy to navigate and, once I got into my stride, the weirdness and difficulties of the past couple of days began to evaporate.

I always remember the feeling that I used to get as a kid when submerged in nature, a sense of peace and calm that overtook me when I was in the woods. I used this as a way of coping with the difficulties that home life threw at me. Perhaps the nature of being in any forest is that you can't see very far ahead, only able to deal with what is immediately visible.

Being an only child, not having anyone else in the house around my age to talk to about what was going on with mum and dad, was difficult. Friends were there sometimes, but the woods, paths, streams and birds were a constant, an everlasting tap of serenity.

Or so I thought until today.

The woodland either side of the path was dense and dark, the dull weather creating a gloom that accentuated this feeling of impenetrability.

After a mile or so, my body began to tell me that it wasn't used to all this activity, and it needed fuel to carry on. I hadn't eaten since the previous evening but unthinkingly hadn't got any food from Ami to bring along. Throwing the rucksack down on the side of the trail, I decided to see what it contained.

The old leather straps keeping the rucksack closed had been oiled and were shiny and soft to the touch. I pulled open the drawcord and took out the contents, placing them carefully on the leaf covered ground.

What I found inside was:

- A very old and strangely annotated map with oiled leather cover
- Small metal flask (filled with unknown liquid)
- The blanket I had used in *'Green'*
- A lightweight metal tube, full of biscuits
- A leather sheathed knife (very old, very sharp!)
- A packet of wax candles
- Cooking pot/metal cup
- Soap
- A leather pouch of light Virginia tobacco, and a silver 'Zippo' lighter, (thanks for encouraging a bad habit, Ami!)
- Small glass vial sheathed in metal and labelled **'Wintergreen'**

I was concerned that there wasn't a tent or sleeping bag included in the rucksack, although I should have guessed by its weight.

Popping open the metal cylinder, I examined one of the biscuits. They were heavy and had a faint aroma of cinnamon. The taste was quite unknown to me, but not unpleasant.

Incredibly, after eating one biscuit, my hunger was gone!

I unscrewed the flask to see what it contained, but as it was metal, I couldn't see a colour. The aroma was minty; pouring a small amount into my metal cup, I could see the liquid was clear. The taste was quite unexpected; the warmth and richness of the flavours made my head spin with delight. I wanted to finish the flask, but something told me that I needed to save this liquid for leaner times.

Feeling surprisingly refreshed, I shouldered the rucksack once again and began following the path between the autumnal trees. It was still relatively early morning, and the thought of a day's walking pleased me. Thankfully, I had chosen to wear my old but comfortable boots when leaving home, so I felt prepared for any terrain or weather this trek might give me.

The path was soft; leaves of the past year pushed into mud from my footfall.

The trees either side of me seemed to encourage me forward. *('Go on, go on, Jack, you know it feels right.')*. The path continued onwards; the day began to awaken and get into its stride before the hours would once again move towards the inevitable dimming of the day.

Rustling.

To the left of me, I heard a noise that was jarring amongst the normal woodland sounds.

Suddenly I felt afraid.

The woods that had been my comfort seconds earlier became sinister and dangerous. I stopped and peered into the dense undergrowth next to the path; I could hear something moving, probably a mouse, or a bird scrubbing for worms. Just as I was about to move away and resume my walk, two yellow eyes appeared at ground level.

'Holy crap, what the hell is that!', I mumbled to myself.

Cautiously moving closer, I began to make out a form in the tangle of undergrowth. A bundle of fur was visible, along with impressively sharp teeth, and a low menacing growl.

'A cat!', I said, to no one in particular.

Feeling slightly baffled but amused, and relieved that danger was not near, I bent down to get a closer look. The tortoiseshell cat was still partially obscured by undergrowth. It was not of the domesticated kind; it was larger and looked quite powerful, its haunches as thick as a man's forearm. It looked at me....no, stared at me with malevolent yellow eyes.

I wondered why the cat hadn't run off? It was then that I saw the fishing twine wrapped around its forepaws. The poor creature had been snared in a primitive homemade trap!

The cat's eyes were searching me; I couldn't walk away from him. The line had made deep slices into the flesh, which I noticed now was bleeding.

Taking my rucksack off, I reached into it for the knife I had seen earlier. Unsheathing it, I tentatively moved towards the growling creature.

'Steady on, old fella', I mumbled to it, looking into its eyes, searching for some sort of understanding of my intentions. The growling, deep and mournful, continued as the knife reached the line. I moved slowly, just managing to get the tip of it under the line where it was cutting into the leg of the animal.

I was uneasy as to what was going to happen next but with a sense of purposefulness, I flicked the knife point upwards, releasing the line from its grisly wound.

The animal hissed and looked, first at me and then down at its unconstrained, but wounded flesh. I gently moved the line away from the other leg and bunched the tangled nylon in my hand.

The cat licked its wounds a couple of times before darting off back into the woodland, leaving a smattering of bloodied leaves behind it. Sheathing the knife, I peered into the copse for a glimpse of the cat but all I could see was the sombre interior of autumn woodland.

Relieved to have helped the animal, I still felt unnerved and started humming to myself as I began my journey once again.

The noise from my footfall on the autumn leaves, and my humming, almost drowned out the human voices that came into my consciousness.

I was unsure as to where they were coming from, but something told me to hide; I stepped off the track and lay down in a very wet hollow as I listened to try and determine their origin.

'...Let's just fuckin' get 'im and get out of this place, it's giving me the creeps... 'e just wants 'im roughed up a bit, and we need to check the traps as well...'

From my vantage point in the undergrowth, I could see the boots of two figures. Both had calf length black laced boots covered in mud, which were plastered with straw and chicken feathers…

'Fucking Ada! Hicks, the trap's bloody disappeared'

'Whadya mean disappeared? Use yer bloody eyes fer Christ sake, will ya!'

'Gone...it's bloody gone I tell ya...whatever it caught, it's bloody dragged it off to God knows where! Look, there's blood and shit on the leaves here...and look...footprints!...he's here somewhere!... Fuck me, 'e'll be furious! We better find 'im and duff 'im up a bit otherwise we are for it...'

The boots trudged off up the path I had just come from, and I saw two retreating figures both dressed in camouflage army fatigues, one slight of stature, the other the size of Oliver Hardy. They were carefully studying the wood either side of them as they retreated, looking for…well…me?

They were obviously not trained in the art of tracking, as they would have noticed that my boot prints led in the opposite direction to which they were heading. I thought it wise to get moving, using their ignorance as an advantage.

I decided to get off the track, as it was too open, and use the woodland as cover. The only issue was that I began to lose sight of the already faint path.

I walked for about three hours. The path that I had been on had well and truly disappeared and I used my sense of bearing, however poor, to keep me in the same direction.

The woods were dense in the area I was walking and, although I knew I was in one of the more populated parts of Kent and habitation could not be far off, I felt very alone.

Twinges of anxiety arose in me when I thought too much about the situation which had unfolded in the past few hours.

Unexpectedly, the scene in front of me transformed; the usual sight of grey dank woodland was changed into a bright, warm sunlit vista as the sun streamed through the canopy above.

Finding the most sunlit spot, I once again took the rucksack off and sat down, using my jacket as a barrier between me and the damp ground and resting my back against a large tree.

The sight in front of me was stunning.

The sunlight had lit the small clearing in a way which brought images of faery rings and folk tales from my childhood. There seemed to be an abundance of wildlife here, and I briefly spotted bright coloured birds that I could not name, flashing in the mystical light.

There was even a cluster of Fly Agaric mushrooms enhancing the magical quality of the clearing.

My eyes closed, and I must have napped for a while, the sun on my face satisfying and rejuvenating after so many dull October days.

I awoke with a weight on my chest.

When I opened my eyes, I was greeted with the floppy ears and grey fur of a still warm, but very dead rabbit on me.

I jumped up in alarm, the creature flopping to the ground. The rabbit lay on the earth, its dead eyes creepily lit with the rays of sunlight still playing through the tree canopy.

‘Holy crap, what the hell is this place all about!’

Even then I realised I had been talking to myself a lot this day.

Movement in the bushes.

The tortoiseshell cat moved slowly and with some trepidation towards me, and on reaching the rabbit sat down with one paw resting on what I presumed was his kill.

The yellow eyes searched me.

‘Hello matey’, I said, ‘what have we got here then, lunch?’

Yellow Eyes kept his gaze on me; it was then I noticed how much damage the fishing line that I had cut away had done to him. The cuts were quite deep, but more worryingly the wounds now looked infected.

‘That looks painful, Yellow’, I said to him.

The eyes never left me.

I remembered that in my rucksack was an ointment of some kind. Rummaging around, I found the small vial labelled **‘Wintergreen’.** I had little idea of what Wintergreen was but supposed by its odour that it was probably in there for some curative reason.

The liquid smelled how I imagined the forests of Switzerland smelt; piney, refreshing and clean. Dabbing some of the liquid onto my handkerchief, I gingerly moved towards the cat I had hastily named *'Yellow'*.

'OK mate, let's see if we can do this without you ripping my arms to shreds.'

Visions of my arm lacerated by the cat's fearsome teeth and claws briefly raced through my head.

The cat continued to stare at me as I moved my Wintergreen soaked handkerchief towards his injured paw.

'Easy now….'; the cat, still eyeing me with the intense yellow eyes, allowed me to dab some of the liquid on his paw.

Only the slightest movement could be traced in his body when the liquid touched the wound. Becoming more confident, I began to wipe away the dried blood, allowing some of the Wintergreen to seep into the raw flesh. I was amazed that the cat placed so much trust in me after his recent experience of human cruelty. I wondered about the trap and whether it was meant for other prey. Whatever the reason, this place wasn't all pleasantness.

I left the cat licking the wounds and thought about how I was going to deal with the rabbit. The thought of a good hot meal was very appealing.

I had never butchered an animal before, so dinner was going to be an experience, one that I thought I may be repeating over the coming days.

The knife in the rucksack lived up to all expectations; the keenness of the blade was more than sufficient to deal with the rabbit. The fur came away easily and, after some trial and error, I soon had the animal hanging above a small fire on a makeshift spit, with the juices dripping onto the flames, creating a wonderful aroma and an expectation in my stomach. The cat also seemed interested in my procedure; the yellow eyes hadn't left me during all the preparations.

For the remainder of the day I walked, contented, with a full stomach, but now wary of the surroundings, for fear of encountering the likes of the two I had seen earlier. The terrain was muddy woodland; decaying leaves on the ground, when trampled releasing aromas of my childhood, memories of bonfire night and drunken parents sending unreliable rockets into the crisp night air.

As days were short at this time of year, I began to think about finding a place to camp. I found a leaf covered dell deep in the woods, crowded with many trees; I felt edgy as the sounds of day changed into the more ominous echoes of night.

The birdsong had now ceased after roosting, and the call of a distant owl added to my anxieties. I spoke sternly to myself, realising that this scenario would be played out many times over the coming days.

Sleep came.

A full belly, and a day of more exercise than I had done in ages, allowed me to drift into a slumber, wrapped in my old combat jacket and covered in the magical blanket from *'Green'*.

Chapter Seven

Raving memories. The walk continues.

I did see Jenny again after she disappeared. Or, to put it correctly, I convinced myself I had.

From the time she disappeared, her family made some effort to cope but the strain of her missing from the home, and the initial press intrusion, finally pushed her parents over the edge. Their already brittle marriage split, and they moved away.

I heard that her father had turned to drink and died lonely in a hospital north of the border.

Her mother died shortly after, having spent some time following the divorce in a psychiatric institution.

It was the 1980s and rave culture had swept the country, allowing the youth of Britain to ignore its troubles by finding a field or warehouse and getting 'loved up' on Ecstasy and bottled water.

The early days of mobiles and the internet made the communication and organisation of these events easier and quicker than it had ever been. Huge numbers attended, and the police found it difficult to manage the drug dealing and trespassing that was part of the scene.

I was a casual observer to this; I viewed the rave culture through the blinkered eyes of a folk enthusiast. I preferred the music of Irish fiddlers or Appalachian banjo players to the techno wall of sound that the rest of the youth sought.

However, I wasn't immune to the whole scene. The genre crept its way, in a somewhat diluted form, to the radio and into the top twenty, which we all religiously listened to on Sunday evenings. Then, of course, it was pumped out of the jukebox in the local pub.

We were all now in our twenties; life was unfolding in front of me, unfolding in the way that I didn't want it to. I could see years and years stuck in jobs that I loathed, in a village that was smallminded and dull.

My friend's parents either showed an all-consuming interest in their children's futures or were indifferent and uninterested. We, of course, were the ones ultimately in charge of our own destinies but at that time, it didn't feel like it.

I guess we were never shown how.

As we all stumbled collectively from pub to pub, filling our bellies with beer, we began to work out that we were shrinking as a group. Some of the lads met girls, and for a time, or for good, they disappeared. There was still a hardcore group that met, almost nightly, and we continued to meet in the pub, and talk the talk of young men, trying to work it all out.

After the pub closed, we staggered back to our parents' houses. Cold kitchens and cheese sandwiches were clumsily made to fill our beer hungered bellies. It was here we individually, or on occasion collectively, made fuddled plans for the future.

It was on one of these unremarkable, beer fuelled nights that Mark celebrated his forthcoming marriage to Karen, the local butcher's daughter.

The pub was filled with familiar faces, the atmosphere was good, and the rounds were getting bigger as more people came in from the balmy summer evening to wish Mark happiness. I can remember that as the hands on the clock drew nearer to 11 and the inevitable closing bell, I didn't feel ready to go back home.

We had all heard that there was going to be a rave not too far away, in a field alongside a main road. It wasn't until the time got nearer to the bell, ('time for walking, not talking!'), that the massive 'thump' of the PA started to be felt in the street outside the pub. It was as if a heartbeat had started up in a neighbourhood that had been needing CPR for a long time.

The beer had emboldened us, given us an appetite for more amusement. 'Let's go to the rave!', someone said, although it feels certain to me now that we would have gone anyway. Before too long, a few of us made our beer fogged way towards the boom and thump of the event. It was a 20-minute walk, enough for us to begin to sober up slightly.

The gigantic marquee was bathed in multi-coloured lights and lasers, illuminated from the inside like a psychedelic womb.

I recall that there was a fee to pay, demanded by 'Hi-Viz' security heavies with shaved heads and powerful torches. Being light on cash after the pub, several of us managed to find a dark spot in the tent's skirt to wriggle under.

The sound was not so much deafening but all encompassing; your whole body was part of the tremendous throb of the pumped-out music. I had never experienced this. My familiarity of local gigs visited with friends was volume without quality, ear bleeding, guitar drenched pub rock. This music, however, was primeval, hypnotic and if I'm honest a bit scary. It was the heartbeat of the new youth. I hadn't used Ecstasy, and there was a tangible wall between us, me and the loved-up ravers that were cocooned in chemical love.

Ecstasy had allowed the opening of consciousness, the music was sacred in its power, the DJ godlike on his pallet pedestal.

I had entered the tent from the outside world by crawling under the canvas skirt and surfaced in the middle of a group of people with unfocussed and glazed eyes. They had beatific smiles etched on their faces, and bottles of water clamped in their hands. I felt lost and out of place.

The beer was beginning to wear off, along with my courage.

They paid me no attention as I danced on the outskirts of their group; they danced to the hypnotic rhythm. I felt alone and out of sync. I was lost in the noise, light and atmosphere, and isolated in the church of the new age.

Just before I decided to remove myself from the tent, I locked eyes with a girl who, although dancing, seemed not to be part of the group she was amongst. Although the light was poor, I noticed that there seemed to be a longing in her eyes (or I wanted there to be, I couldn't tell now, this night was so screwed up). Her eyes seemed to be saying 'get me out of here', although her body was synchronised with the other zombie like dancers.

Whether she understood my indication I don't know, but I nodded to her, then towards the outside of the tent and, (rather foolish it must have seemed to the dancing circle I had adopted), dropped back under the canvas skirt and into the outside air.

The night was heavy with mist, and the ground below my scrabbling hands was damp to the touch. I felt the knees of my jeans begin to soak up the mud and moisture from the earth. It felt good, a grounding from the weirdness I had left behind.

She was already outside the tent on my exit. There were no awkward silences; she spoke to me straight away, leaning in to my ear, 'Let's find a quieter spot'.

I was naïve, as these sorts of encounters did not typically happen to me. I had no idea why she wanted to find a 'quieter spot' but my instinct told me not to question.

We wandered across the dewy grass in silence; the music was too overpowering to hold conversation. I restrained myself from staring at her as we walked, for fear of scaring her off. Instead, I looked down at my sodden desert boots, taking in glimpses of her bare legs emerging from a filmy flowery mini dress, resolved with military boots; a style I had not seen before, but loved immediately.

We came across a tree with fairy lights strewn over the trunk and branches. As they twinkled in the night air, her skin and hair were fleetingly illuminated, creating glimpses of elfin like beauty.

I looked into the night sky as we sat under the tree; lights and lasers filled the air, and the early morning mist made the night sky seem ethereal. She reached out and held my hand; energy surged through me, and my senses were suddenly overloaded. Aromas of jasmine and patchouli drifted around us; I momentarily wondered if my senses were deceiving me, as I associated these scents with the tree fayres that I usually visited during the sultry summer months.

We embraced to the monotonous 'thump' of the rave music enveloping the night.

To this day, I can't recall who initiated the embrace. It seemed to be borne from the senses and the heady mist-soaked air; earthy, sensual and intoxicating.

We made love in a field close to a major arterial road, the thump of music the soundtrack to our hunger, the roots of a tree the bed of our joining. Over the years I have tried to recall the intimacy, the words, the movements. I can't. No conversation had really passed between us since we had met, no introductions or niceties. The one thing I do remember from all those years ago was the cry she gave as she climaxed. She cried my name. The name I thought I had not told her.

I trekked home eastward that night, walking along the road that several years later would see me travelling in the opposite direction, in a camper van produced in the same year I had experienced rave music and 'met' Jenny again (or so I had convinced myself during the intervening years).

'*Yellow*' and I continued our walk through the woodland. He was not always in view, but I was beginning to sense his presence just beyond the pathway, stalking through the undergrowth or fleetingly crossing my path. Our routine continued for a few days, never varying. After I had a fire lit and got my sleeping arrangements sorted, '*Yellow*' often brought a rabbit to the camp for dinner, once a squirrel!

He would leave me after eating, but when I awoke in the morning, covered with the night's dew and aching from the previous day's walk, he would be next to me, staring at me with his baleful yellow eyes.

This arrangement continued for several days.

The woodland walk was never varying, and I was surprised at how few signs of life or habitation I came across in my travels. I was beginning to get into a sort of rhythm, and my body began to complain less as I put on my boots for another days hiking. My thoughts about home were diminishing. (In retrospect, years later, I wondered if this was part of the spell that the trees and nature were weaving on me).

Once again, I awoke to yellow eyes and a covering of dew on my blanket. I breakfasted on water and a couple of biscuits from the tube I had found in the rucksack.

As I began to walk on this particular morning, a feeling of apprehension followed me.

I felt anxious and, although the path was clearly defined, I began to worry that I was lost or going in the wrong direction.

The map that Ami had eventually relinquished on our parting, although ancient, did show some landmarks that I had recognised on my journey; mainly boulders with old chunks chiselled out of them, now full of moss and lichens.

Most of the day passed without any incident, although the feeling of dread followed me along with my yellow furry companion. I hadn't seen or heard the two fatigue clad men from earlier, but I was still uncomfortable and jumpy. After several rests, the day began to lose its vibrancy and the beginnings of late afternoon brought the inevitable twilight.

It was the smell that confused me at first.

It was a smell that took me back to my childhood; I couldn't place it immediately as there was another underlying smell that had a sort of malicious suggestion alongside it.

Candy floss. Sweet, pink, tooth rotting Candy floss. It was a syrupy, cloying smell that I remembered from visits to the seaside, and the fairs that used to turn up in our town every summer.

As I walked further along the path, the surroundings began to change from the dense woodland that I had become accustomed to.

The trees became less impenetrable and more of the immediate surroundings could be seen. There were trees that were thin and willowy that I couldn't identify.

The patchy grass, although heavy with water at this time of the year, seemed darker and more like the grasses I had seen in my visits to the north of the country, where bog land forced grass to adapt to its peaty soil.

'Yellow' seemed to have disappeared for a time, although I assumed that he would be near. It had become more difficult for him to hide now the shrub land on either side of the path was sparse.

My anxiety increased as the smell became more overpowering to the point of making me feel nauseous.

The terrain began to open the more I walked; in the near distance I could make out a small rise in the land with what looked like a circle of trees on the summit. The cloud cover was quite low and the scene in front of me changed every minute. The only thing that stayed constant was the smell, which with every step became stronger, increasing my apprehension until I could feel my heart pounding under my jacket.

As I began to climb the hill, my vantage point began to alter. The circle of trees about half a mile away became more distinct. They looked like pines, although they were still shrouded in cloud, and I could now make out their distinct spire like shapes.

Light had begun to fade, and I wondered where I was going to be making camp for the night. The obvious choice was at the summit of the rise in the circle of trees, although my feelings of disquiet didn't fill me with hope for a restful night, and the smell of candyfloss was getting stronger.

From the misty scene in front of me, I thought I saw a figure exit the circle of trees and begin to walk down towards me. The light was now so poor I wondered if my mind was playing tricks with my senses, but no; a figure *was* beginning to come towards me!

Chapter Eight

Carnies and Candy Floss

As the figure drew nearer, my fear dwindled. The image rapidly appearing in front of me was one of a child-like man, difficult to put an age to him, dressed in what appeared to be an amalgamation of country gent and circus clown.

His jacket and trousers, both generously cut, were of bright yellow with contrasting brown stripes. A shirt of electric blue with ruffed collar was complemented by a red bow tie.

His footwear was black boots, covered generously in mud. The ensemble was completed with the strangest hat I had ever seen.

It was in the style of a bowler but seemed to alter colour and shape the more I looked at it; it also seemed to have various fabric 'flaps' in it which opened and closed as he walked. I might have been imagining it, but I could have sworn there were glimpses of eyes from within the flaps!

'Felicitations to you, young man!', he cried, in a voice which I can only describe as discordant and high pitched, much like a penny whistle played by a novice, all squeaks and air.

'Er…hello', I replied. Not having spoken to anyone for several days, my voice sounded odd in my own head.

'Do you wish to partake of the Fayre?', he exclaimed, with some exuberance. He pronounced fayre with the old English inflection.

'I'm not really sure', I replied, 'what sort of Fayre is it?'

'The best! We have Freaks, Freakishness and, of course, Girls!'

After this explosion, I certainly saw the bowler hat's flaps open, and winking eyes looked at me, quickly disappearing behind the fabric flaps once again.

'Well, I'm not sure, I need to rest up. I'm a bit tired as I've been walking all day.'

At this, the strange creature jumped up and down in glee, laughing and clapping his hands.

'Tired he is, tired and weary, he says! Come to the Fayre and refresh, come to the Fayre and make new friends, come to the Fayre and meet old friends!'

'Incredibly and certifiably crazy', I thought to myself. However, the idea of human company and a rest was tempting.

Nodding in agreement but with some hesitation, I followed the now leaping and jumping strange man-child up the hill towards the promised delights.

As we approached, the smell of candy floss increased but so did the underlying smell that I couldn't place earlier.

It now struck me that the smell was similar to one I had encountered years ago when I had visited the vets with our sick cat.

Fear, blood and death.

Anxiety increased once again.

Soon, the fayre began to emerge from the dusky light.

Electric coloured bulbs cast a glow over the grass and tents, a petrol generator adding to the cacophony of smells and sounds. My eccentric guide could be seen ahead of me, and beckoned me with, *'Come to the Fayre, it's all free today!'*

I entered through an unattended turnstile. His words of encouragement reminded me that I had heard a similar phrase before in a sinister setting, but for the moment I couldn't place where. He then disappeared into the chilly dusk. The fayre seemed disquietingly devoid of many other people. In fact, I was becoming increasingly aware of being almost alone.

I had no idea as to where the fayre was situated. Was there a town nearby?

Those few that were in the fayre grounds were wandering around, silent and unnaturally solemn. They seemed almost ghostlike. I began to notice that there were no children to be seen amongst the adults.

I suddenly remembered where the phrase the strange man had uttered earlier had come from.

'Ice cream, lollipops, all free today!'

My anxiety grew further as I walked through this oddly placed fayre. It somehow seemed that it was all staged for my benefit.

The path through the fayre led towards the Big Top, and my weary legs carried me to the entrance. There was a torn, flapping poster advertising the show inside. Hand painted and crude, it simply said:

THE GRE TEST S OW ON EARTH

No usher to welcome. No sound from within. No hum of expectation from spectators. I pushed open the canvas flap and walked inside.

As I entered, I could make out a sawdust ring, churned and rutted, and littered with animal faeces, making the smell even more intense. A single yellowed carbon arc spotlight played high up on the canvas roof as if it were an artificial moon. The original odour I had noticed outside grew stronger, making my unease increase. I turned to walk out, but a metallic voice rang out from the darkness through a bullhorn:

'Hey, Jacky boy, don't go...we have a show!'

Hoisting the rucksack a little higher, I turned and ran back towards the open tent flap in a blind panic.

I recognised that voice!

The way out had now disappeared into the gloom of the tent; my eyes hadn't yet adjusted from staring at the spotlight. I needed to escape; I wondered why I had come to this place at all! I should have listened to my apprehension and kept away. As I ran, my foot caught on a peg hammered into the ground. I fell with a mighty *whump*!, knocking the air clean out of my lungs and sending a worrying bolt of pain up through my foot.

It may have been my imagination but as I fell, I could have sworn I heard raucous laughter as if on a TV comedy show. Canned and corny.

(Canned and corny...just like you Jacky boy!)

Looking up from my vantage point on the damp muddied ground, I could just make out the entrance flaps.

They had been securely closed, seamlessly knotted and fastened with white rope. I was going nowhere for the time being.

'Oh dear, Jacky boy, face down in the mud, eh? Just like school, eh?'

The voice. The voice of the school gate, and the voice of the petrol station. The voice I had been destined to hear again.

I always knew it would speak to me once more. I just didn't know when it would be. I knew now. Turning my head with trepidation, I saw on my left a pair of red work boots with turned up blue jeans resting on them. The leather of the boots looked wet and glutenous.

Red.

Cloying.

Red.

Blood.

Blood seeping up the jeans.

A word from school hit me. Osmosis.

'Well Jacky boy, why don't we get the show started, eh? It's been a long wait for both of us, hasn't it?'

I tried to look up at the face speaking these words, but my position on the ground didn't allow me to.

I then became aware of the arc light. I could still see the tent's sloping canvas gable, and the super trouper playing on its side, but now there was a focal point. A cage; a cage with a woman inside.

Tenderly, I was lifted up, and a chair was placed just outside the sawdust ring.

I was gently led to it. Slowly and compassionately I was lowered down, a surprise after the violence I had expected. The only things I had in my line of vision were the arc light and the girl enclosed in the cage.

Tinny music began to play through metal horn speakers, music of the kind heard in 1950s holiday camps. It was something military and marching like Souza. The cage and arc light began to lower and, when it reached the sawdust, I could see the figure inside with more clarity.

A hand remained placed firmly on my shoulder as I sat in the chair, not reassuring but insistent. Metal handcuffs had secured me to the chair. I turned my head to look at the hand on my shoulder. All I could see were calloused fingers, one of which was adorned with a huge silver ring.

A fetid odour hit me as my captor knelt beside me and spoke, letting out his putrefying, rancid breath.

'Well Jacky boy, she looks radiant does she not? You do recognise her though Jacky, do you not?'

Gazing at the harshly illuminated form, I saw several things at once.

The first was red hair, although this looked to be dull, thin and fragile. The second was the unnaturally sinewy body encased in a tight-fitting bodysuit.

The third was the most disturbing.

Jenny was full of fun. Not in an always laughing, annoying way, but in the way that when you were with her, she made you feel special and alive. Her smile was so bright it created shadows. To this day, I have never met anyone like this. She listened to your problems. I mean, really listened. Whenever I was sad due to Mum and Dads' arguments, she always knew, and took time to listen as I told her all that was on my mind.

It was rare that she used to unload any of her problems on us. Anyhow, she was a girl, and I guess we assumed that she had girlfriends that she could offload on.

One day, it was different. Jenny arrived at the camp with her trademark cap pulled just slightly lower than usual. I was the only one in camp, and was just reading one of my beloved American comics, wondering about the possibilities of ordering the Charles Atlas bodybuilding course, or X Ray Spex - **'See thro' Clothes with ease!'**- *accompanied by an illustration of a curvy woman in corsets!*

Jenny sat down next to me, picked up a discarded comic and pretended to read.

I knew she hated comics, so I realised she was just going through the motions, trying not to distract me. Of course, I saw through this.

I put my comic down and looked at her sideways. Just below the peak of her cap, I saw a white bandage, stained reddish-brown with dried blood.

'What happened to your head, Jenny?'

'Oh, it's nothing really, just a cut from tripping up and hitting my head on our mantlepiece.'

Jenny had turned away from me while she mumbled this. I didn't believe her, of course. I couldn't remember if she even had a mantlepiece.

I left it a moment.

'So, what really happened Jenny?'

She looked directly at me and I saw something different in her eyes. Something I had never seen in her before.

'Jack, you and I are best friends, aren't we?'

'Of course,' I replied, 'the very best for forever!'

'Well, you know that what I tell you stays with us, right?'

I nodded in affirmation, and replied, 'Right, yes, of course!'

She began speaking hesitantly.

'Well, yesterday on the way home from school, I got in a bit of a fight.'

I was ready to defend Jenny and knew that while she had very few enemies at school, there were some girls who were jealous of her quiet, assured ways and popularity.

'It wasn't with anyone in school, Jack', she stated, as if reading my mind. 'I was walking along Dark Lane and this weird guy began to follow me. I tried to get away from him, but he was quicker than me and he grabbed me and….'

She bowed her head, and I saw a tear fall onto the blue of her dungarees.

'He knew me, Jack. And worst of all, I knew him. He has been in my life since I can remember. He's in my thoughts, dreams and visions constantly. This is the first time I have actually seen him though. So, he grabbed me, and I struggled, and I kicked him, and he yelled, and he punched me. He must have been wearing a big ring or something because I got cut bad. Felt like it went to the bone, really made me feel sick. I told Dad that I was in a fight at school. He got mad and, after putting this bandage on, sent me to bed. That's it really.

Jenny didn't want to say more; I guess it was too painful for her. I didn't ask. I wondered at the time why she hadn't told her Dad it was an adult that had attacked her?

But they were different times back then, times when adults were always right. Even the abusers. Like Mr Finch.

Years later the conversation in the camp haunted me as I thought about her disappearance.

The other thing that was a constant reminder of that awful day for her was that every time she looked in the mirror, she saw the scar that the episode in Dark Lane had left on her.

...the third thing was the scar. A scar partially hidden by thinning red hair and badly applied stage make up.

The cage was an old-fashioned iron type, like the ones used by the great escape artists of the past. Cylindrical, steel barred, and locked with an oversized keyed padlock.

Jenny was slumped in the cage. I wasn't sure she had seen me or recognised her old friend. My heart lurched. After so long, she was only feet away from me. And alive!

Without trying to understand the gravity of the situation we were in, I knew that we were both in peril and somehow needed to get out of this surreal theatre. It seemed to me even then it could have been derived from the nightmarish imaginations of Bosch or Bacon.

Before I could solidify my thoughts about escape, the voice from my own nightmares rang in my ears.

'Well Jacky boy, let's get this show on the go, eh? We haven't all the time in the world, you know!'

With this exclamation, the figure of my childhood dread lifted himself into view.

Nothing had changed since those early years. The bulk of his frame and the jowly, sideburned face remained as ridiculous and terrifying as they did back in the schoolyard of my youth. Liberal use of black hair dye had badly covered the 1950s rockabilly hairstyle. A very poorly fitted red ringmaster's cape hung on his frame, lending the surreal situation an even more bizarre air.

He walked over to the cage and, with a bunch of keys attached to his belted waist, inserted one into the padlock and swung open the heavy barred door.

Jenny made little effort to get out of the cage. She was either too weak, drugged or scared.

'Come on girly, rehearsal's over. Showtime! OUT!'

Jenny lifted her head and began to crawl feebly from what I could see now was a filthy and squalid cage. Our eyes met as she began to creep over the sawdust on her hands and knees. I didn't even know if she recognised me.

From a gap in the ring, a small figure emerged pulling a heavy chain. As the figure moved closer, I could see it was my greeter from earlier on. He walked towards me.

'Told you! Welcome! Felicitations! We have Freaks! Girls! And........'

... a roar exploded from behind him.

A lion, shabby but huge, was lumbering towards the cage, encouraged by the eccentric figure pulling a chain which ended in a collar around the beast's neck. The man-child repeatedly glanced nervously back to check the lion's progress. The bowler hat had now taken on a life of its own, with the fabric flaps opening and closing, and the eyes all wide with fear.

With the use of an extendable metal pole, my captor, the ringmaster, walked confidently towards the lion, who cowered in his presence, and by placing the pole on top of the lion's huge head, removed the clasp holding the lengthy chain. The lion was now free to roam.

Jenny, as if on cue, and who also seemed to cower in the ringmaster's presence, walked up to the lion and knelt in front of it.

'Now Jacky boy, now you will see a show! A show that you have never seen the likes of! A show that you have been waiting for all your life!'

The ringmaster turned towards me, his eyes boring into my soul and his mouth grinning in a perverse smile.

Turning back towards the lion, and Jenny, he gave a signal to the bowler hatted man-child. Using a similar metal pole as the ringmaster, the man-child touched the pole to the lion's flanks, making it cry out in the most bloodcurdling, yet sorrowful, way. As the lion roared, Jenny put her head fully into the creature's huge mouth. The lion kept his jaws fully open, his eyes staring balefully and mournfully at the metal pole being wielded by the man-child.

The ringmaster turned to me and through a megaphone ranted:

'THIS IS THE MOMENT, JACKY. THIS IS THE TIME YOU AND I HAVE BEEN WAITING FOR. TIME FOR YOU TO KNOW ME. TIME FOR ME TO GET TO KNOW YOU EVEN BETTER!

'IN A FEW MOMENTS JACKY BOY, THE GREAT LION TAMER MISS JENNY WILL BE NO MORE! SHE WILL MEET HER DESERVED END WITH THE BEASTS SHE LOVES!'

(Canned applause and laughter from the dimness of the stalls)

'I WANT YOU TO KNOW WHO I AM, AS MISS JENNY HAS FOUND OUT WHO I AM OVER THE YEARS, JACKY BOY. I WANT YOU TO KNOW WHO I FULLY AM, BEFORE YOU GO THE SAME WAY AS MISS JENNY, JACKY! SO, BEFORE WE START, LET ME TELL YOU MY NAME. IT'S IMPORTANT TO KNOW YOUR EXECUTIONER'S NAME, EH?'

(Mutters of audience agreement from the speakers)

'SO, HERE I AM. HERE I STAND, JACKY BOY. I HAVE HAD MANY NAMES OVER THE YEARS. BUT TODAY I STAND BEFORE YOU AS ***TOBIAS PONTIUS RUM, AT YOUR SERVICE, SIR!'***

Before I could muster a reply, or even think about the situation both Jenny and I were in, the ringmaster held up the metal pole, and with a theatrical flourish triggered it to emit a bolt of white electricity which surged towards the central pole of the tent.

'I will not be thwarted again, Jacky boy!'

I quickly looked at Jenny, whose head was still in the lion's mouth.

The man-child was now sending numerous charges of electricity through his pole, aimed at the lion's flanks. It wouldn't be too long before Jenny would be hurt. The lion, whimpering, even with open jaws was beginning to relax its huge mouth on Jenny who kept her head in place as if in a trance.

'Jenny, for God's sake, get out of there!'

(Oohs! and Aahs! from the 'audience')

As if on cue, the lion reluctantly began to close his jaws. Even in my distress, I could see that this was more through defeat and fatigue than aggression. Jenny made no effort to remove herself from her situation. Her red hair was now soaked in saliva from the beast's mouth. Man-child was jumping up and down in joy, as he could see the imminent outcome to the situation and used the pole with ever more frequency, making the beast's fur singe, adding to the concoction of smells in the arena.

Another smell began to permeate the tent, one that I could readily place from my childhood...

During the clement months, our 'gang' often camped out overnight in the den. There was a beauty to the night sky, the way day changed into dusk and then to the darkness, bringing to light the ceiling of stars that roofed over our heads, a welcome change from the dreary bedrooms of our homes.

There were times when the weather was not so good, so we had managed to club together our pocket monies and buy a small canvas tent which allowed four of us to sleep inside.

On one of these occasions, another boy from school had overheard our plans and asked if he could join the sleepout. It didn't seem much of a problem to us at first. Ian wasn't a bad kid; he had a younger sister who was often in trouble at school and Ian used to try to defend her, consequently getting into trouble himself.

We made camp that Friday night in October. The air was chilly, and we spent much of our time chatting and playing 'war.' This involved two groups who hid from each other in the nearby sand works pit, using whatever weapons they could find to fight, homemade catapults being the most popular, made using chunky elastic bands stolen from the school library. It was all pretty good natured; no one ever got seriously injured apart from the odd bruise or cut.

We never worried too much about injuries; we were more scared of the man who used to run the quarry.

If he caught a glimpse of us, or his evil dog barked a warning, he used to give chase. So far, we had never been caught.

Dusk crept over the day and a fire was made, sending embers and sparks into the clear air. I remember that there was much laughter that evening. Ian was doing impressions of some of the teachers in the school and Jenny was pretending to be the naughty child, uncharacteristically backchatting in return, something she would never have done in real life.

As night fell, the subject of ghosts and horror inevitably came up. We had all passed round 'The Pan Book of Horror 4' (stories selected by Herbert Van Thal). A popular read at that time, it had fuelled our imaginations and coloured our conversations around the campfires. We were just talking about the covers of the books, which seemed gruesome at the time. Number 4, our favourite, had a Victorian doll on it - scary enough - but to really make the point a large spider was crawling over her!

Other voices apart from our own infiltrated the night air. Before too long, murky faces appeared from out of the woods, faces we recognised from school, but the names escaped us. This was not the case for Ian, as one of the boys addressed him and Ian replied using his name. Before too long, it became apparent that Ian had blabbed about the whereabouts of the den and the planned sleepover.

The whole feel of the night changed as the newcomers joined our camp. The conversations had a sharper edge to them, and an uncomfortableness fell over me. To make matters worse, they had brought beer with them, and were beginning to become louder and more boisterous, kicking the fire and throwing lit twigs into the woods. One of the boys took out a bag and produced two small gas bottles, ones that were used for attaching to primus burners. In retrospect, the events that followed were obviously pre-planned, and undoubtedly Ian knew something of what happened next, as we never saw him around our circle again.

The campfire burned with a ferocious heat, as it had been fuelled by extra wood that the new boys had slung on to it. With a primal scream, the boy with the gas bottles threw them directly into the hottest part of the fire. For what seemed like an age, none of us registered the gravity of the act.

Then pandemonium broke loose as we all ran, tripping over each other as we grabbed our possessions and sought safety. The boys ran along with us, as we all looked for cover. It seemed to take ages for anything to happen as we ran but after a couple of minutes there was an enormous WHUMP! as the camp was surely blown to pieces. Orange embers lit up the night sky.

We spent a good deal of time making sure that no sparks had set any of the surrounding woodland alight.

Jenny was more than distraught. She always hated any kind of violence and remained quiet and tearful as she painstakingly checked for any signs of fire.

We made our way back to camp. Our tormentors had disappeared now, along with our beloved den. We could see that our tent had not fared well; it had been badly scorched and, although not on fire, was smouldering in places, giving off a smell similar to burnt paper or leaves…

…the tent was on fire!

The metal pole that was central to the tent's structure had conducted Rum's electric current straight up to the apex of the canvas, and it was now beginning to smoulder, with smoke clearly visible as it was suctioned down and lit up in the ever-present arc light. I was helpless.

The tent was on fire, Jenny had her head in a lion's mouth, and I was handcuffed to a chair. Apart from that, my foot hurt like hell from where I had fallen.

Sometimes in life your senses are overloaded. The first time you go to a speedway or banger car race. The noise of the vehicles, the smell of the burnt fuel mixed with fried onions, and the sight of psychopaths battling in a circle of dirt and dust. The tent was like a speedway event. I struggled to remain grounded.

And yet, even with all the stimuli, something else was nagging at my already overloaded senses.

Fur.

Looking away from the chaos ensuing all around me, I glanced down. Familiar fur and equally familiar eyes were viewing me inscrutably.

'Yellow'!

As if under starters orders, no sooner had I recognised my trusty companion - how could I have forgotten him! - he bounded off directly into the ring and leapt, claws extended, onto and into Rum's back.

'You fuckin' bastard, you fuckin' Jimmy shit in a pail bastard furry turd!'

'Yellow' had hit the spot, no doubt there, but with this outpouring from Rum came a sweet surprise. Jenny seemed to be released from her captive trance and managed to stand up, much to the dismay of the man-child, whose bowler hat was now in overdrive.

'Let's get out of here, Jenny!'. My words were obvious but urgent.

'Yellow' was making good work with Rum.

He had him on the floor now with his fearsome claws at his throat. *'Yellow'* and the lion appeared to be communicating with each other with deep growls and higher pitched yowls, and the large beast was now making a slow but sure goal of Rum.

'Jenny, grab the keys from Rum and unlock me!'

Out of her daze now, Jenny bent to Rum's belt, and while he was occupied with claws and impending mauling, Jenny unclipped the bunch of keys and bent to my padlocked wrists to free me from the captive's chair.

As I was about to hug the emaciated woman I had thought about for my whole life, a greater urgency was upon us. The whole of the upper tent was ablaze, the canvas dropping burning cinders onto us and the sawdust floor.

'Jack me boy, Jack, get this furry shit beast off me lad! I promise no harm will come to you or your lassie ever again, please Jacky me boy this creature is going to slaughter me!'

'Fuck you Rum, and your promises! Good luck to you, I hope the beasts eat their fill of your wretched body! Let's get out of this, Jenny!'

We ran, or in my case stumbled on my injured foot. Grabbing the knife from my rucksack, thankfully undiscovered by Rum, I sliced the retaining cords securing the tent and we escaped the outlandish circus.

I felt torn as I stumbled away from my prison. I had left my faithful companion behind, along with however many beasts Rum had kept secured in his perverse show tent.

But we escaped, and I had Jenny with me.

We spoke no words as we stumbled away and down the hill I had climbed only a short time earlier. Moments later, it seemed safe to stop and regain our composure.

The night was beginning to diminish into day and, as we looked back to the tent and the fayre, we could see it was encompassed in thick white smoke, the pungent smell of burning canvas wafted down the hill on a gentle breeze.

'Oh my, Jack, those poor animals! And your cat...it was your cat, wasn't it?'

'Yes; well, in a way. He sort of adopted me after I got him out of a fix. One of Rum's fixes, I think.'

As we gazed at the remains of the fayre, the white smoke began to disappear and fade. The view was replaced by a thick mist which quickly rolled down the hill toward us in the dawn of a new day.

Chapter Nine

Part the Second. Jenny's Story

The day I went missing was, in all respects, a perfect day. A day of friendship and clear cobalt skies viewed through towering green pines.

The joyful sound of laughter about nothings. The smell of the woods coupled with woodsmoke and the rich smells of baking, chip fat and dampness that hung on our clothes from our respective homes. Two-ounce paper bags of sweets, (cola and pineapple cubes, sherbet pips, and sweet peanuts!), bottles of Cresta, (*'It's frothy, man!'*), and the gross smells that the boys produced, seemingly on demand.

I had never been happier.

Life was always good with friends, but friendship coupled with my time in the woods was constantly a mystical and meaningful experience for me. Jack and I could talk for hours about how we would make bigger camps in other woods, in places we had only heard about from magazines and the few TV programmes we watched about other countries.

Whenever a programme was on about the American state parks or the Canadian wilderness, we would talk for hours about how we would survive and live off the land. There was once a programme about Alaska, and we made childish plans to go there when we finished school at 16.

Only five years away!

I had been damping the fire down when the boys left. They thought it was because I didn't trust them to do it properly, but the reality was that I liked to spend a few moments alone in the woods, without the noise that a large group created.

As the fire began to diminish, I hopped up onto the rope swing we had thrown around an oak bough that summer.

I can remember the peacefulness that swept over me as I swung back and forth, thinking about the long hot summer days ahead, playing with my friends and having fun away from the troubles of school. I pulled my precious yellow baseball cap down over my eyes as I swung, letting the wonderful disorientation and dizziness wash over me.

'When the bough breaks the cradle will fall...'

A pair of arms encircled me from behind, stopping the motion with an abruptness that was shocking.

At first, I thought it was one of the boys playing a trick on me, and I laughed nervously, asking them to let me go. I realised with dreadful suddenness that none of them would be tall enough to do this.

'Well, what do we have here, then? Little Jenny nature girl, is it? Little meddling Jenny nature girl, knows shit all 'bout nothing. Well girly, you are going on an adventure now, but not with your darlin' Jacky boy!'

It was then that Rum, (although I didn't know him by name then), lifted my cap and threw it into the woodland, catching part of my hair in the rear metal clasp and ripping it from my skull.

He hoisted me up, and with one huge, ringed hand clamped over my mouth, carried me struggling, (futile as he was so strong), out of the woods and into the back of a truck that was parked on the edge of the woodland in a narrow lane. The noisy clang of the lock engaging, as I was thrown into this metal jail, rang through my whole body and stayed with me for a long time.

I didn't know it then, but I was now enslaved in the service of Mr. T.P. Rum.

In the hours, days and weeks that followed, I was driven around in the back of the locked truck. God knows where we were most of the time; my prison was windowless. I was allowed out only infrequently, and always shackled in some way. His methods were ingenious, and there was never any opportunity to escape.

I shared my claustrophobic space with many things during the travels: barrels of chemicals, medical supplies and waste. The list was endless.

The worst, though, were the live animals which Rum collected from different locations. They were usually caged and in a very poor state.

I was treated coarsely by Rum and his underlings. There seemed to be several with whom he had dubious connections, and two of these characters remained with us constantly as we drove around the country.

One was called Hicks.

He was obese and had a sadistic streak which often came to the fore when any punishment needed to be dealt out. This was the case in the early days of my confinement as I hammered on the side of the truck until my fingers bled, hoping someone would hear me.

Hicks just came into the rear of the truck and, without saying a word, grasped a piglet from one of the pens and slowly squeezed the life out of it, as he brought the poor creature's head closer to mine, so I could watch the life go out of its terrified eyes.

He was always very cruel to the animals and seemed to get great pleasure from hurting them while I was looking. I learnt not to make a noise for fear of his relentless brutality.

The other was Lenny, who was the muscle man of the outfit. He changed tyres and mended the old truck if it broke down.

I didn't get on with either of these two thugs, but I was always more fearful of Hicks because of his unpredictability and cruelty.

As time slipped away in this awful situation, I became ill and lethargic. I had sores on my buttocks from being bounced around on the thin mattress in the back of the van, and the lack of natural light was taking its toll on my physical and mental health. Although Rum showed no sympathy for me, for some reason he didn't want me to die just yet, so one day he told me we were going to get some sea air.

The day started as brutally as any other, rough driving and the awful darkness that was only ever broken if the rear doors were opened for loading or unloading. Then we stopped, and as the doors swung open, bright glorious daylight haloed Rum's badly dyed hair.

'Let me tell you this, little girly. One wrong move and you end up like the little piggies. You with me, girly?'

I nodded. I remember thinking then that there would be a wrong move; I would find any opportunity to escape.

Yes, Rum, a wrong move was definitely on the cards!

Unsteadily, I got out of the truck onto a gravel path which seemed to be part of an industrial estate. It could have been a Sunday, as I couldn't see many cars in the car parks next to the factory units.

It must have been about midday; the sun was fierce, and I missed my yellow baseball cap. I remember getting upset about this. I tried not to cry, but a tear escaped my eye. I made sure Rum couldn't see it.

Rum led me down the path which eventually led to a large green area. Then the smell of the sea! It was like nectar to my senses. We walked along the green clifftop, which was high above the water, the cliffs stretching as far as the eye could see. I made out sailboats and ships further out on the horizon.

Oh, if only they knew my plight and could take me with them on their voyages! There were other people, but not many, going about their business and enjoying the sunny day, completely unaware of this girl who was imprisoned by a madman.

Rum never explained to me why he abducted me that day. He didn't need to, really. We both knew.

Ever since I was young, I knew that I was somehow different to most of the others I hung around with at school.

Apart from Jack, of course.

But Jack, although the same age as me, hadn't quite reached conclusions about his own 'gift.' Although at times it didn't seem like a gift. It seemed like a tremendous weight that hurt. There were times when others were enjoying themselves and I was emotionally chaotic.

The annual trip from school caused much excitement for weeks in advance. Last year's trip to the National Portrait gallery in London had been a disaster for the school.

Most of the children had taken the opportunity to eat their packed lunch and most of the sweets and fizzy drinks they had brought along, in the first half hour. There was sickness and bedlam on the coach, (run by the local coach company at a discount price), as the usual problematic kids threw sandwiches and beverages around the vehicle.

As the smell of vomit began to reach the nostrils of the elderly driver, he pulled over and refused to drive any further until the vomit was cleaned up.

The firm refused to use their coaches for any future trips, so this year a new company with more modern coaches stepped in. They must have heard the story from last year, the only modern thing we could see was a sick bag resting on every seat.

This year's trip was to a zoo. One of the biggest in the country, it boasted animals from all over the globe. The coach was full of excited children, ready to spend their pocket money on plastic and furry toys from the gift shop. We were split into several groups, I was put with some of the louder children, to even things up I guessed. Miss Ratenburg, who was one of the nicer teachers in the school, led our group.

It was a lovely hot day, although being a redhead I was conscious of my already burning skin. We really hadn't got very far into the zoo before we came to the monkey enclosure.

Chimpanzees were lethargically trying to climb the wire mesh, or poking fingers through the holes to take food from the visitors. I can remember the hilarity of the children that surrounded me, as they shouted insults and taunted the caged monkeys.

I became aware that mentally I was inside the enclosure with the chimps, but it was also as though I had been bodily transported. Just like the TV programme Timeslip, I had crossed a barrier.

It was the first time that I had a powerful sense of the injustice towards animals that humans wielded. The 'gift' of acute and crushing empathy had begun, although it was a word I was unaware of, as yet.

The jibes and insults toward me suddenly became intimate. I became uncomfortable in my skin, and felt my face beginning to flush. One of the chimps met my eyes. There was a connection. It was as if it was pleading with me, asking me for something, something my young mind struggled to understand.

But a deeper shift had occurred, and from that moment my connection with animals and people changed forever.

One of the children, I can't remember who now, threw her sandwich at the wire, hitting the chimp in the face. I punched her straight in the nose. I wouldn't react that way now, but it was a potent moment in my life.

Rum and I walked along the cliff top. To any onlooker, it could have been father and daughter spending some quality time together.

'I need to use the toilet, Mr. Rum.'

He'd asked me to call him Tobias, but this felt too intimate, too friendly. I vowed, even as the years passed, I would remain formal. Up ahead, I could see a small refreshment hut, the kind you only get at the seaside.

'Girly, you better get in and out of there quick. You make a sound with this' (Rum made a theatrical gesture with his hand across his mouth), *'and your precious piggies take a holiday with Hicks. Got it?'*

All smiles, Rum guided me into the hut and got direction from the woman behind the counter as to where the toilet was.

As I came out of the toilet, Rum thanked the woman and we began to walk out of the door, but she called, 'Hey, little girl. Looks like you are burning up there. Do you want some sun cream, or a hat?'

'She's fine, we are going back to the car now.'

Rum was in a hurry, the uncomfortableness in his manner was evident.

The woman had other ideas and, before Rum could react, she grabbed my hand and led me to the rear of the hut, telling Rum to 'stay put' while she applied lotion to me.

Gently and tenderly, the lotion was applied to my face and arms, the first time in a long while that any sensitivity had been shown to me. A tear formed in my eye.

'What's your name, dear?'

Nervousness washed over me, as my awareness of Rum just a few feet from me made me hesitate with my reply.

'Jenny'. I spoke softly and made no eye contact.

'Jenny? Funny, when you walked in, I thought "here comes Jenny", how odd! Mine's Deborah, lovely to meet you, Jenny.'

I was acutely aware of Rum's proximity and, when the lady began to ask me more questions, he walked over and grabbed me by my arm and once again made his way toward the door.

'Thanks ma'am, mighty obliged we are, for sure.'

'Bye Jenny, try to stay out of the sun!'

With that, my normal human interaction ended once again.

I turned and smiled at this wonderful lady.

As my head turned back towards the door, something stuck to the window caught my eye. A sun-bleached flyer, held by three brown, perished Sellotape strips, barely legible, faced into the café:

MISSING!
HAVE YOU SEEN THIS GIRL?

There was a picture of me taken about three summers ago, yellow baseball capped and smiling at the lens. Underneath, some details and a phone number to contact. I wasn't sure if Rum had seen this, but we were making a very hasty return to the truck, and he seemed mad.

'Diddly fuckin' sun cream shit on your face! Want some sun cream, dearie! Meddling two faced piggy bitch, I know her kind!'

I smiled inwardly remembering her words:

'Funny, when you walked in, I thought "here comes Jenny", how odd!?'

Like Rum, I could have barely imagined the turn of events that day. As we walked back to the truck, his mood began to improve, and he began to tell me of his plans for me in the future. I must have been about 14 now, and he told me that I was old enough to begin to work with the animals he had purchased to start his circus. He knew, of course, that animals and I had a kinship with each other. No doubt this would work in his favour when he needed them to perform his ghastly tricks.

As we neared the industrial park, I could see that there was a lot of commotion around the truck. Two police cars were parked, and several officers were looking around it.

Before Rum had a chance to react, I bolted off toward them. My legs turned into jelly as I ran with all my might; I feared Rum's hand would grab me at any moment. I dared not look back. All I recollect is running headlong into a police officer, and when I opened my eyes his blue serge jacket was covered with sun cream.

'I'm sorry, I'm so sorry', I sobbed, 'please don't be angry!'

They never caught Rum.

He disappeared; he was very good at that. Hicks and Lenny had also disappeared. I can remember that a huge countrywide search went on to try to find them. But I knew that they were hidden and cloaked by dark forces, some within the system, and they would never be found.

After I had been placed in one of the many foster homes, (none of my extended family wanted me), I returned to the hut on the cliff to thank Deborah for her quick-wittedness and kindness.

She was not there, but another waitress told me what had happened. She told me that Deborah had taken her own life on this clifftop, about a year after she had saved me.

Shortly after I had been rescued, a man had become a regular caller to the hut; and in particular to see Deborah. The waitress told me that he seemed nice at first but appeared to have some sort of hold over Deborah. After Deborah died, she never saw him again. I asked her what he looked like.

'Large, very large. A bit like that funny man. You know the one. The one with the skinny one, that's in the old films....'

So, I had a few years trying to get myself together. I went to school; I caught up pretty well. The nightmares continued, and I saw a counsellor. It helped, but you don't recover overnight from the sort of treatment that Rum inflicted on me.

I became a vegetarian and became interested in animal rights and the environment. It seemed right somehow, as if that was my purpose. No, it was more than that. As if it was my destiny.

Then I met Ami.

She was my heroine. It was as if everything I wanted to be was encapsulated in her. It wasn't just the clothing, although she was cool! She had ideas, philosophies, and wasn't afraid to live them out. She seemed older than her age, as if she had existed on earth previously.

We met when we were 17, both attending the same sixth form college, both studying art, both bored and frustrated with our peers.

It was after we had been hanging out for about a year that she told me about *'Green'*, and the will of earth to survive, and the determination of man to overrule this. It took me a while before I could believe her. But she was convincing with a quiet wisdom. It just 'was' with Ami.

What persuaded me to believe her, way before she finally took me to *'Green'*, was her knowledge of Rum. Although it wasn't Rum the person she used to speak about, but the mannerisms, personality and volitions of the person she described that finally swayed me. It transpired that Ami had had dealings with another 'Rum', albeit not so extreme as my encounter.

Ami was someone that totally understood my fears and anxieties from my experience with the dark part of humanity. It was so good to have a real friend that understood me.

Ami never spoke over me. I became aware that often I had been speaking for hours, and she was just listening. She had always tried to convince me to see Jack.

I spoke of him often; I just couldn't bring myself to contact him. There was too much ground to cover and I was afraid things wouldn't be the same as they had been in the past. In the past, when we were kids. In the past, before my childhood was stolen, along with my girlish dreams.

Ami and I had arranged, in the summer of my twenty first year, to attend as many festivals as we could. We had become festival addicts, our favourites being the Tree Fayres which were run by lovers of nature and music, no corporate influences allowed! I was working on an arable farm during the day; menial work, and low wages, but I was in the great outdoors. It suited me completely.

Money was an issue, but festivals were our life. We made our funds stretch.

The rave scene was in its infancy. It wasn't something that I was particularly interested in; the music was fine, but the chemical fuelled happiness, and fake comradeship, seemed at odds with my growing philosophies.

But here we were. Back near my childhood home, in a huge marquee filled with loved up people dancing, in small groups, to huge beats and anthemic music.

They bore expressions of ecstasy, fuelled by small chemical pills and tabs. The profound loneliness of these smiling loved up people spoke to my increasing gift of empathy.

This wasn't Ami's scene either, but I could tell for some reason it was important that we be here. She was always curious about what turned the young on. In retrospect, I guess it was to understand, more fully, the way the youth were heading, socially and spiritually.

The bass was pounding through my body. I tried to relax and join with the communal ambiance, but I felt stiff and awkward, dancing on the edge of a group of strangers.

But Jack was there.

He wasn't hard to spot. Like me, he was a fish out of water in this canvas tank. Like me, he was trying to attach himself to an oblivious group of fluorescent clad ravers. Like me, he looked out of place in combat jacket, jeans and desert boots.

Strobes and dry ice made any prolonged eye contact difficult, but Jack was making signals that he wanted to meet me outside. I'm not sure he even knew who he was beckoning to.

Chapter Ten

Jack, Jill & Jenny

As the mist descended the hill, Jenny and I covered ourselves in the blanket that was attached to my rucksack.

'What a lovely warm blanket, Jack. I am so cold!'

Jenny was shivering and coughing from the effects of the smoke. Contemplating the face that had meant so much to me over the years, I could plainly see the effects of the cruelty and abuse that Rum and his minions had perpetrated on her over time.

'We need to get going soon Jenny, I don't know what is happening up there.'

Looking up the hill behind us, where the mist had eerily covered everything in sight, I imagined supernatural forces at work, ready to employ further pain on us in a short time. I couldn't believe that Rum was out of the picture just yet.

'I can barely believe that I am with you, Jack! I have waited so long for this moment since…(cough)…since that time we briefly met a while ago'.

She smiled coyly at me.

'I don't think I can go on much further. I feel ill and totally exhausted. Rum got what he wanted from me, but I am free now. I couldn't have wished for a more…(cough)… What I mean is, Jack, I couldn't have asked for a more beautiful way to pass from this earth than to be with you.'

I tried to stop Jenny from thinking along these lines, but she hushed me and softly continued.

'There is something very important I need to tell you before it is too late. By now you are surely aware that you are part of a lineage of people who have the quiet ability to change dangerous issues in this world.

'You and others like us bring awareness about the damage man is doing to his home. Remember when we were kids and we used to talk at the den about trees, animals and all that stuff? Tell me you remember that, Jack?'

I nodded in affirmation, smiling at the sweet memories.

'Then you will understand that, although your life will never be the same again, it will be rewarding, and so needed by the Earth. I hope you have as much passion for her as when we were young, Jack. Do you?'

Again, I nodded.

'We need to go soon, Jack, but not far. There is a *'Green'* not too far from here. Do you know where we are?'

'I have a map; it's old but…'

'We are in Sussex, on the Sussex Downs, a beautiful place. We need to find two windmills; I don't think they are far. Shall we go?'

I lifted her up, stowed the blanket, and with one last look back to the mist covered hill that had fulfilled my worst nightmares, started to walk.

'One more thing, Jack. When we get to the windmills, we need to get 'married'.'

I stopped and looked at this wonderful woman.

'I'm already married, Jenny.'

She looked at me and smiled. 'Not in the conventional sense, Jack.' She began to chuckle through wheezing breaths. 'I think it would make our daughter happy!'

A few moments after Jenny had uttered these words, the meaning sunk in and when I was able to form coherent words again, we began to walk slowly along, reminiscing about our childhood and picking up the pieces of our stolen past.

The winter sun broke through the mist and blessed us with some warmth, albeit feeble. Jenny held my hand and sobbed with delight when recalling the time we had spent together at the rave. How she knew that she had conceived a girl, and how she had told Ami about it on the way home; how Ami had been ecstatic at the thought of our forthcoming little 'Green goddess.'

She told me how Ami had looked after her during her pregnancy, and then cried, 'Oh Jack, you should have seen her when she was born! She had masses of red hair and was just a delight to be with.

'But the joy of the birth was short-lived, as Rum's dark web had tracked me down to *'Green'*, and although his power was diminished there, once again he abducted me, this time when working on the farm. Fortunately, Jill was cocooned safely in *'Green'* with Ami.

'Those were horrible years, Jack. I missed my daughter so much. My heart broke every morning; I learnt how to be numb when I performed for Rum in his ghastly circus. I never showed him my tears, they were saved for the long nights alone. I knew that Ami would take care of our child, but I was her mother. It cut me to the bone in every waking moment.

'So, I performed in Rum's foul circus most days in the summer. In winter months we travelled around in the truck collecting animals, hazardous waste and meeting shady characters.

'You may be wondering why Ami didn't inform the police, Jack? Well, she did exactly the right thing by not telling them. You see, the police would of course get involved, but Ami and I had often talked about what would happen if I went missing again.

'We both felt that by trying to reach out to you, there would be a better chance of things being resolved properly by someone who understood the forces against us. Anyhow, not only is Rum elusive, he also has influences that spread deeply into the fabric of our society, so there would be no guarantee that he would be prosecuted for his wrongdoing.

'So, you see the 'chance' meeting you had with Ami in the pub, although you may have thought coincidental, was in fact engineered by greater forces than we can possibly imagine! It goes back to our love of nature and the communication the trees have with each other. It all goes back to the den, Jack! Only one good thing came out of that period though, Jack. Rum was unaware of Jill. Until now.'

Jenny was becoming more animated in her speech as we walked further from the scene of her rescue, but I could tell by the way that she was walking that her energy was low, and that we would need to stop and rest for the rest of the day and, probably, night.

The Downs were becoming more extreme in their undulations as we climbed high hills and descended deeply into chalk lanes, leaving our footwear white, as if walking through snow.

There were few trees and, for the most part, the Downs were sparse, apart from scrub and gorse. As we ascended to the summit of one hill, we came across a stunning view; far in the distance the sea sparkled like a diamond tiara. Directly in front of us was a ring of Beech trees, perfect in their geometry, and incongruous in their location.

'It's the Chanctonbury Ring, Jack!'

Jenny was quite obviously excited to be here, although I couldn't really understand why.

'The trees were planted by one of our kind. In 1760, a chap named Charles Goring planted them. There was a lot of opposition at the time; people said they spoiled the Downs. But he did it for a reason. A bit like why we put mobile phone masts up now; they were a means of communication.'

As we moved nearer, I could see that the trees were not closely planted. There was a presence about the location that was otherworldly.

'Some think that the ring has supernatural power, Jack. An author slept the night here once and recorded a very disturbed night. Probably best we don't dwell on that now, though. Are we going to sleep here tonight?'

I could see no other option, but it was a perfect spot; there was no wind, and the day had been remarkably mild. Moving into the trees, I found a clear patch and began making camp while Jenny rested her back against a tree, humming an old tune I couldn't quite place. I felt tired and worn out after the day's exploits, and my foot needed resting.

I found some Tippler's Bane mushrooms growing in a shady spot, and over a small fire cooked and ate them with Jenny, along with the remaining biscuits from my tin.

'Tippler's Bane, Jack? They are delicious, but I never heard them called that!'

'Well, in the rucksack Ami gave me was an old notebook tucked away in one of the pockets. Must have been left there by the previous owner. It's been quite useful really. It lists the plants, berries and fungi that are edible or poisonous. I found these listed under edible mushrooms, but you can't have them with any alcohol as you get very ill, hence the name. I think most people know them as ink caps.'

'Have you any Wintergreen, Jack?'

'Yes, Ami put some in my rucksack, I've used it a few times on this journey. I even used it on Yellow.'

Talking about this made me think about my old companion and his gruesome fate. Unexpectedly, fatigue overtook me and, lying my old army jacket down, I lay on the leaf covered ground. Jenny removed my socks and boots, and gently rubbed the healing liniment into my tired and damaged feet. Before I could thank her, the warmth from the lotion seemed to envelop my whole body and I fell into a deep and dreamless sleep…

…and woke up screaming in terror.

A darkness had shrouded me, and something was pushing down on my chest making it difficult to breathe. I struggled to pull the blanket down away from my eyes, to see my assailant more visibly. Freeing myself from the entwined blanket, I raised my arms ready to pound my attacker.

My hands found the source of my distress, a heavy creature covered in fur. I seized it ready to begin a fight, but through laughter Jenny called out for me to stop.

My assailant was in fact already deceased. A very dead rabbit.

And sitting next to me, in the morning blurriness, two yellow baleful eyes stared into mine.

My heart pounding, and my body flooded with adrenaline, I sat up and laughed along with Jenny.

'Thank you, Yellow! Good to see you, old friend!'

Gingerly, I reached out my hand; *'Yellow'* allowed me to stroke his head, and then padded a few paces over to Jenny, climbed onto her lap, and closed his eyes as she rested against the tree giggling.

'Oh Jack, after all you've been through, you are scared of a dead rabbit!'

'Looks like you have a friend as well, Jenny.'

'Oh, he's lovely, Jack, and he survived the fire, and Rum! If only he could talk!'

'Yep, that would be helpful, I'd like to know if Rum survived, or if he is maimed for life!'

'Oh, Jack, I hope not. I detest him, and hope he gets punished, but I can't wish that on him'

'Well, you are a better person than me, Jenny, and I suppose you are right, but knowing where he is now would sure make me feel happier.'

With dawn breaking, we broke down camp, and once again walked the white chalk paths towards the awaiting windmills.

We walked slowly as two old people would; Jenny was worn out, and her cough had worsened. *'Yellow'* followed at a distance; he carried the rabbit in his mouth, probably wondering why we had not eaten his gift. He periodically stopped, taking gruesome bloody chunks from his kill.

'So, what is it with Rum and the whole circus thing? When I arrived in Kent, he, or one of his underlings, left a load of flyers advertising it.'

'It's a cover, Jack. You see, while I was with him, he used to travel all over the country with the show. But really, he was more interested in the places we visited. They were normally out of town, down on their uppers sort of places; there he could meet and convert the disillusioned in life to believing his warped philosophies. That's apart from the peddling of drugs, animal trafficking, disposal of medical waste…. need I go on!

'What are his philosophies then, Jen?'

'He believes in raping the earth of its resources for his own profit, and the gain of others like him. His line goes back a long way. When Ami and I lived in *'Green'*, we did some research about his ancestry, as much as we could.

'Their lineage goes back a lot further than we could research with our limited resources, and we were constantly being hindered in our enquiries by converts to his cause. We found that they had even taken the words of scripture from the Old Testament and used it for justification to meet their own needs. Remember the verse from Sunday school in the Bible, Jack…'

"Be fruitful and multiply and fill the earth and subdue it and have dominion over the fish of the sea and over the birds of the heavens and over every living thing that moves on the earth."

'Well, that was only part of the story. They used any means they could to convince people that man could, and should, deplete the earth because that was what was written in whatever religious text or philosophy that fitted for the time, or situation. It was really borne out of selfish greed and intolerance of other ways of thinking though, Jack. Through the ages, Rum's kind got involved with the occult and supernatural forces.

'Over time they became stronger; the Nazi movement owed a lot to them. They were, and are, ruthless when challenged by groups of environmentalists, or those trying to preserve what is left of a broken planet.

'Even local councils have members of Rum's kind. Well-meaning folk were threatened, or just quietly disappeared when their voice became too strong. Hence the reticence of common folk to get involved with the big issues like saving the planet!'

'But when I was at *'Green'*, Ami told me that the earth itself was speaking. What did she mean?'

'There are so many things you need to know, Jack, but this is not the place to talk about that. We are out in the open; who knows if Rum is still abroad? Once we get to the windmills we can rest and talk!'

As she spoke these words, in the distance the twin windmills came into view, and we stopped talking and focussed on the haven that we needed so badly. One was circular, the other four-sided with a domed top. This, Jenny told me, was Jill.

The wind was keen now and the Downs began to appear sullen and unwelcoming; it would be good to be indoors. I was concerned for Jenny; she was pale and weak, and her cough was becoming more prevalent, although she didn't complain. We needed a hot meal and good rest, and I hoped that this was the place where we could get both.

The windmill was as white as the chalk path that led to it. Left derelict for many years since its construction in about 1765, it had been restored to its former glory by dedicated volunteers. Little did the visiting public know of the parallel history it hid beneath the still revolving sails.

'The windmill is a good cover, Jack; we can enter through the main entrance but there is a small trapdoor that leads underground. That will be our home for a while!'

And so, for the first time in days I walked through a small wooden door with the promise of a meal at a table, and a bed not under the stars, but underground!

So, with chalk encrusted boots and shoes we walked into the ancient windmill called 'Jill.'

Chapter Eleven

Bonding and Breaking

Jack, I had a call from an 'acquaintance' of yours. Apparently, you stayed with her after you left me. She sounded young……midlife crisis, Jack?! Well, she went through your phone contacts and found my number and called me to inform me you wouldn't be back. Well, that's fine by me. She wanted a conversation, but I wasn't in the mood. Do give her my love! And do enjoy your midlife crisis, Jack.

By the way. I was visited by a nice man who said that he knew you from old and was keen to make contact again. I gave him your phone number. I hadn't heard you speak about him before. I think his name was Hicks.

Jeanette.

The letter was left propped up on a shelf.

'Well that's quite a welcome'.

I showed the short letter to Jenny who remained quiet then handed it back to me.

'Ami can explain more about this Jack, she probably sent the letter down here. Shall we meet the others? I need a bath, a sit down, and most importantly I need to introduce you to your daughter…. I'm so excited!'

The interior of the mill was brick lined, contrasting with the white wood exterior. The floor was fitted with old pockmarked polished wooden floorboards, partially covered by a heavy looking and bright oriental rug.

'Jack, help me lift this up. We can get to the trapdoor and go down to the living area.'

We descended steep wooden steps which led down into a surprisingly well-lit cavernous space. As my eyes became adjusted to the artificial lighting, I could see an old woman sitting in an old wing back armchair looking down intently at a screen.

'Hannah!'

Jenny ran toward the woman who looked up with a serene smile on her face.

She didn't rise but putting the screen down on a side table, opened her arms to Jenny who knelt to hug her. For some time, they embraced while I looked on.

Eventually Jenny rose and with tearful eyes addressed me.

'Jack, meet Hannah, she is one of our oldest and wisest allies.'

I moved towards Hannah noticing for the first time how ancient but uncannily youthful she looked. She had an orange shawl wrapped around her, long silver hair tumbled over it, shining with a lustre which must have taken hours to achieve.

'Hannah remembers the mills being built Jack, how wonderful is that!'

I couldn't comprehend what Jenny was trying to convey to me at this point as, unexpectedly, I found myself on my knees hugging Hannah.

'We've been expecting you, Jack, it is so nice to see you!'

'Thank you', I replied clumsily.

As I rose, I glanced at the LCD screen that Hannah had placed on the table.

The screen was a topographical map of the world with red dots scattered all over it, with red lines running between the oceans and the land.

'This is how we monitor the life of our Mother, Jack', Hannah said, nodding at the screen.

'Mother Earth is dying in our hands; we use this technology to gauge where events need our attention. You probably thought we talk to the trees, didn't you!', Hannah giggled in a quiet way.

'She's playing a game with you, Jack', Jenny whispered, 'she has a wicked sense of humour; of course, we still talk to the trees!'

It was at this point that Jill walked into the room. Jenny walked over to her, beckoning me to follow. There were no words. We had all been absent from each other for so long, there was so much to say, and, in a way, the past seemed inconsequential at this moment. We joined in an embrace that seemed to voice all the stories we had to offer one another, and for the moment, we were satisfied.

Jill and I looked at each other and we both shyly smiled. There was a lot of ground to make up.

Jenny took to her bed after a wonderfully satisfying meal. She looked pale and drained but was clearly overjoyed to have her family surrounding her. Jill and I sat around a glowing electric fire, talking about anything that came into our minds. We said nothing of any great importance about our current situation.

Hannah remained quiet during our talks; she was absorbed with her screen but several times I noticed her nodding and observing me when I spoke.

'We use the windmill for power', Jill said. 'We have a bank of batteries at the back of this room that stores our energy. We use the electricity to run our lights, heating and computers. It's best for us to be off grid so we can't be traced and avoid any awkward questions from the authorities. The windmill trustees are totally reliable and onboard with our mission.' As if to assert this statement, I heard the wind increase and the huge sails creaking overhead.

Hannah moaned and slumped even further into her chair.

'What is it, Hannah? Are you OK?'

Hannah passed the portable screen to Jill.

'Oh fuck…sorry dad…you don't mind me calling you that, do you?'

'It feels strange, but I quite like it! What's wrong?'

'We've lost another connection. You see the red lines crossing all over', Jill said as she passed me the screen.

'They are the communication channels that this app allows us to see. The red lines are the general communications between trees, animals, fish, birds and pretty much all wildlife. It's based on a very old system that's been around since the beginning of life on earth. We didn't really understand it until recently, it's only just lately that some great minds, with sympathy to our cause, have converted this intricate and complicated system into computer language. The study of trees is becoming more important lately. It even has a name now; they call it dendrology. It has proved very important for us to use as we can monitor the state of the earth, all from a windmill in Sussex!

'The red lines have started to disappear over the past few months, which is a real worry as it means that the earth is beginning to shut down, and we've just lost another major communication across France by the looks of it.'

‘So, the animals and trees are dying?’, I said.

‘Partly true, but our understanding is that they are, by their own volition, turning themselves off.

‘It seems like they have just had enough of pollution, brutality and all the things that humans have thrown at them over the centuries. Last week, a group of us in Sumatra found a whole colony of Orangutans dead at the base of a cliff. It appears they had taken their own lives. It was a horrible, gruesome sight.’

‘Jenny said that when I got here a lot would be explained about the earth’s situation, and I guess that I’m beginning to build up a picture now. But how did this all start?’

Hannah cleared her throat, and in a gentle lilting voice began to speak…

‘Long before man had taken complete dominion over the earth, deep in the forests of Europe lived a man and woman. They, along with others in the village, were nothing out of the ordinary, and lived an uncomplicated life, dwelling in a wooden structure built into the forest itself. They breathed a routine existence. Pietro went out every morning into the forest to collect wood and hunt for food.

The winters were very fierce, and a warm fire and full belly were essential for survival.

The forest was a dangerous place in those days. There were many wild animals, also trying to survive the elements, and Pietro was always wary of travelling too deep into the forest, especially on the short winter days.

Sophia stayed indoors. She was an expert in weaving and used her talent to make clothes and blankets for the community, as well as for Pietro and herself. It seemed no one could replicate Sophia's skill in weaving, and her blankets had the unusual property of being very light but also wonderfully warm. She used dyes that came directly from the forest plants, and Pietro was often given instructions to bring certain plants back from the forest for Sophia's dyeing.

Sophia was known throughout the community as the kindest and most wise person. She spoke little, but always had a listening ear or kind words to say when needed. It was often the case when someone in the community fell sick that Sophia knew which herbs and plants would ease the condition. In the depths of winter, she took to feeding the small animals and birds from her hand, her red hair tumbling down over her wonderfully colourful coat, which seemed to change colour with the differing seasons.

Pietro and Sophia were childless.

They dearly wanted children, but year after year Sophia remained barren and they both quietly carried on with their lives, each hoping that the following months would bring better news.

On one desperately cold and overcast day, Pietro once again set off into the forest to hunt food. The forest had been reluctant to offer any game for many days now and all the men in the community spoke of hunger. They feared that their families were going to struggle over the coming weeks if food was not found. That day, Pietro broke the rule he had stuck by for many years. He ventured past the old oak which was the unspoken boundary of his hunting grounds. He walked deeper and deeper into the forest, his senses keen for any animal he might sight with his bow.

Soft snow began falling in the dimming light and Pietro became afraid. The forest was now unknown to him, and he saw strange plants and trees that were unrecognisable. Then, out of the corner of his eye he saw a fleeting glimpse of a creature moving in the distance.

Pietro raised his bow and sighted in the direction of the vision. Then he saw the beast. It was as large as a bear, but hairless and seemed to use animal skins as a crude covering. Its head was human, but larger than Pietro had ever seen.

Pietro hesitated.

He couldn't kill a human! Although this creature was obviously not human in the sense he knew. The beast moved towards Pietro. Pietro couldn't run as his legs had gone to jelly and his bowels had loosened in fear.

The beast spoke to Pietro. Its voice was guttural and low, but perfectly audible, even with the wind blowing through the trees. The beast offered him unlimited game from this part of the forest.

Whilst the creature was speaking, animals began to appear all over the forest and in the air. Birds, squirrels, hares, deer and boar began to walk without timidity close to Pietro and the beast.

With a strange laugh, the beast offered Pietro to try his bow.

The arrows flew as Pietro killed scores of animals to take back home to Sophia. Under the beast's gaze, he filled his gunnysack to the brim with his slaughter.

The beast promised that he could return every day and kill as much as he wanted. There was only one condition. Pietro was to bring his firstborn into the forest on its 10th year.

The beast wanted to teach the child to hunt and give it the skills in enticing the animals of the forest. Pietro agreed, as he knew that it was unlikely that Sophia would bear a child, and the thought of so much food was too good to be true.

Pietro trudged back to his abode under the heavy weight of his gunnysack. When he walked through the threshold into the warmth, Sophia rushed at him, deriding him for staying out for so long. Pietro laughed and showed her the contents of his gunnysack. Before Pietro could react, Sophia picked up the plentiful sack and rushed out into the cold dark night. She distributed the contents throughout the community, to the great joy of the receiving families

On her return she found Pietro in an uncharacteristically bad mood. He chastised his wife for carelessness with his bounty, saying that he had killed it and wanted it for himself and Sophia. Sophia tenderly caressed his tired head and made him sit next to the roaring fire, while she cooked an abundant meal.

It was on this night, with the cold, steel wind cutting through the forest, and the sound of nearby families singing songs of thanks, that Pietro and Sophia conceived their first born. The baby was born the following summer and named Sophia after her mother and grandmother. She had her mother's temperament and demeanour, and, after a few months, her hair took on the red glow that her mother was recognised for.

Now there was a great joy in the household. Over time, mother and daughter became inseparable, as Sophia became as adept as her mother in the skills of weaving and herbalism and so became an invaluable addition the community.

Pietro continued his prolific hunting in the outer part of the forest; he didn't see the beast again, and over time forgot about that winter's day. Pietro became cagey and selfish with his hauls, even allowing his game to spoil rather than share with the community. The dwelling now began to smell of decay and putrefaction as the animals piled high in the parlour. Still Pietro kept all his gains for himself.

With this arrogance came isolation as Pietro's friends gradually ostracised him. Pietro became a bitter and unlikable man, but Sophia continued to love him, as did his daughter who brought joy to her mother but increasing anger to her father who began to resent his daughter, blaming her for losing his friends.

The day before Sophia's 10th birthday, Pietro was out hunting as usual. The day was warm and sludgy, and Pietro felt tired and out of sorts. He had already killed a number of animals but even though he was weary, the bloodlust was in him, and he wanted more.

He sat down under a tree and lit his pipe. As the smoke billowed around him, his eyes began to close and he thought about the earlier times with Sophia, before she was with child, and the good times he had with her and also his friends, all of whom had deserted him now; and a great sadness enveloped him.

When his eyes opened again, the beast was standing before him.

Pietro had all but forgotten about the creature over the years, and once again he became fearful of this strange being. The beast reminded Pietro of the promise that he had made years before and Pietro, being scared and having little feeling towards his daughter, agreed to bring her into the forest the following day.

So, the next day Pietro did exactly what the beast said. Sophia was excited to be with her father; they had not been walking in the forest for many years and Sophia, although wary of her father's bad moods, was happy to be going along with him.

When they reached the edge of the known forest and began walking deeper into unknown woodland, Sophia started to become anxious; she also began to see many plants and trees she did not recognise.

The beast stepped out from some bushes ahead of father and daughter. Sophia jumped behind her father with a cry.

It soon became obvious to Sophia that her father had premeditated this meeting, as he engaged in dialogue with the creature and, without her consent, she was soon taken by the beast away into the depths of the forest.

Pietro waited patiently for the beast to return with his daughter. A great sadness had now overtaken him as he realised the enormity of his crime, and in his head he could still hear the wailing that his daughter made when the beast carried her away.

Pietro remained in the forest all night, alert for any sounds of the beast or his daughter. When the sun arose in the morning, he understood with dread that his daughter would not return.

In his distress and shame, Pietro found the white flowered Hemlock plant and without hesitation consumed a large handful of its flowers. He died a slow painful death as his lungs slowly became paralysed.

So, the woodland flowers robbed one Sophia of a father, the other of a husband.

Sophia began to walk in the forest in the vain hope of finding her beloved daughter. The months passed, and winter crept in once again with its steely fingers. Sophia walked further and further into the forest until one cold overcast day she met the creature. He was caught in a leg trap, probably left by her husband many months ago. Sophia without fear or caution released him, and from her skirts pulled out a small vial marked 'Wintergreen.' With this salve, she rubbed the creature's wound and bound it in clean fern. The creature made no sound apart from pitiful whimpering.

The creature stood unsteadily, turned and began to hobble off back to the depths of the forest. Sophia made preparation to leave but a small glint on the forest floor caught her eye. She picked up a small clasp, the clasp that held her daughter's hair in place after her mother had brushed it to a high sheen only a few months ago. Held in the clasp were two red hairs.

Sophia returned to the forest many times over the following months, but the creature that held her daughter never returned.

Many years later when touches of grey had crept into Sophia's hair, a woodsman from a distant region came to the community. After he had been welcomed and fed by the ever-giving Sophia, he told a tale about a creature that had been seen deep in the woodland with a beautiful red-haired woman who was chained to a travelling cart. He told the villagers about the group of men who banded together to capture this strange beast and rescue the woman. But the creature was swift and cunning and fled in the cart towards the great seas, never to be seen in the forests again.

Sophia continued to commune with the forest; she picked plants and tended wounded creatures when the need arose.

One early spring day, when the first hint of warmth was felt on the cold winter's soil, Sophia sat down to rest with her back on a young oak. She was used to listening to the plants, animals and trees now. They spoke to her as clearly as the villagers did every morning as she left for the forest. As her weary eyes closed for the last time, the young oak spoke to her with wisdom and comfort.

'You have served the forest well, Sophia. Oh, if only all mankind was like you! Be assured that your line will continue, and that as long as it succeeds, we will protect it. Sleep now, join us in the great circle of life!'

With that, Sophia breathed her last breath, in serenity at last.

That evening, a wind blew through the trees, stirring the leaves that lay on the forest floor. They soon covered Sophia in a woodland shroud. The villagers never found her, but those who knew her best recognised that she was in the only place she ever wanted to be.

'I've heard that story many times, Hannah, but it never fails to move me.'

Sitting on the floor below the steps we had come down a few hours previously was Ami.

She had crept in during Hannah's captivating tale and was smiling fondly at Hannah. She turned and addressed me.

'So, do you understand more now, Jack?'

'Well, it was a great tale, but how does this relate to me?'

Ami made a hand rolled cigarette, lighting it and offering me the pouch.

With a roguish look, she said, 'You remember the picture you were looking at when you came in the *'Lynch'*? Well, that was a representation of Sophia, it was painted by this wonderful lady here'. Ami nodded towards Hannah.

'You see, Hannah is a direct relation, many generations past, to the young Sophia who was lost all that time ago. At one point in her captivity, Sophia managed to escape, much like Jenny. The Earth didn't want to give up on one of its own, so the trees, animals and mother nature worked against the beast to allow Sophia to have some happiness for a short while until she, like Jenny was recaptured. But during this time, she conceived, and so the bloodline was able to continue for the benefit of the Earth.'

'How do you know all this?', I asked.

'Why, Jack. The trees told us, of course!'

The following morning, after a breakfast made by Hannah, several cups of freshly brewed coffee, and two guilty handmade cigarettes from Ami's never-ending pouch of tobacco, a meeting was called.

Ami, Hannah, Jenny and Jill all sat around a small round table, with the laptop screen that Hannah was using the previous evening open and booted on the table.

Jenny was the first to speak. She looked rested but pale, her voice when she spoke was frail...

'First of all, it's so wonderful to be with my friends and family. My time away from you all has been a time of great sadness and trial, but even in my darkest times with Rum, I held onto you all in my heart, and I know that you did the same. What can I say to my dear childhood friend and empath, Jack! You were my knight in shining armour, thank you for coming for me, and most of all thank you for our beautiful daughter!'

With tension etched in her expression Jenny continued…

'I have known for some time that things were moving on, and that Rum would be challenged. My precious hope was that I would see my beloved Jill, and Jack again. So, I can only thank you Ami for not scaring him too much…he made it here! I know that you will all guide my dear Jack on the next part of his venture; yes, Jack it's not over for you yet I'm afraid. As Ami has probably already said you come from a line of warriors! Didn't you know?'

(Sniggering from the table at this point).

'Anyway, on to more serious matters.

'Hannah has informed me that one of the ancient Yews in this county, the one tree we rely on for assessing the welfare of all the trees and wild fare in this land, is beginning the cycle to shut down. She has seen it on the computer you looked at last evening. In other words, it is choosing to die. We think this is because of the increased activity of Rum and his cohorts over the past few months. More chemicals and waste have been seen in tankers around the area and we think they are being dumped in the earth near this site.

'When I was on my way here, Jen', I said, 'a tanker pulled up in the petrol station next to my old van. It was unnerving, I think it must have been Rum who spoke to me then; he seemed to know all about me! I think the name on the tanker was D.L Fuels or something like that?'

'It would have been, Jack', said Jenny.

'He's probably been on your trail for some time, and he took his chance as soon as you left the relative safety of home. D.L Fuels, can you guess what that stands for? D.L Fuels is Dark Lane Fuels. Remember the old scary lane, with the creepy man hanging around, on our way home from school? He played on our darkest fears. We should know all about that.'

'Jesus, that's disturbing, Jen. I'm so sorry, the gang really let you down, didn't we?'

'Not really Jack, we were young, remember? How could we understand the enormity of what was going to happen to us? That's the nature of evil, it blinds the good people, because it's so far removed from their experience of life. We must focus on the future. For Jill, and for her children, and her children's children.

'You see, in Hannah's story, Pietro was a weak man. Not inherently bad, but weak, which some may say is just as bad.

'He could have changed the tragic outcome, but greed took control of his spirit and he was then lost, trying to fulfil his needs in more and more killing. Unlike his wife, his body gave no nutrient to the soil in his demise. That's the way it works, the soil has no use for poison in its substance.

'Do you know the story of Pom? It follows the story Hannah told of Pietro and the forest where they both perished. And it also tells of why the trees cannot trust us.

'We can't even trust each other.'

Pom's Story

We had marched for days; my feet were bloody and raw from the wet and cold that the army issued boots did nothing to repel. My wife and daughter were back in the homeland, eking out an existence along with the other villagers in my district on the outskirts of Stalingrad. And now we are marching across the homeland with the Germans nipping at our heels.

The rain is intolerable, soaking our greatcoats and duffle bags, making them twice as heavy.

We were not told of our destination but as we neared another country village, gunshots could be heard way out in the impenetrable forest that quickly became a regular sight to our weary eyes.

Oh, how I ached to be back home in my own forest! It was nothing like this one. Not half as gloomy, and the only gunshots come from villagers like me, hunting rabbits.

How I laughed at my silly daughter who got so upset when I brought the slaughtered creatures back to the house. She is far too sensitive and needs to learn to be tougher like her father!

We make camp again on the outskirts of this new place; Katyn, they call it.

Adrik gets his harmonica out as we finish setting up camp.

In the dark and wet camp, we smoke and drink any vodka we have left, and sing Russian folk songs, along to Adrik's tunes, until sleep takes us away from this hell.

Mornings bring a new hell, as we try to cram our boots on over swollen and bloody feet. The men are worn down and irritable, and cracks are beginning to show between them. Arguments are quickly stopped by the captains who threaten to cut rations or shoot any troublemakers. Tensions go underground.

We are told to get ready quickly as we are being picked up by trucks today. Thank God! No walking for a while, that's some relief anyway. I reach in my pocket for my tobacco, but it is gone! I ask my campmates if they have seen it, but they walk away with strange looks on their faces.

A few days ago, I had an argument.

As we were marching along another dreary road, a dog joined us. Obviously hungry, its bones showing through its bedraggled fur, the dog became a regular visitor, the other men feeding it food we couldn't spare. I voiced this belief but got bellowed down by the others.

A couple of days ago, the dog returned. It did its usual begging routine; this time it hung around my feet, tripping me up on occasion. I became irritated with the creature and swiftly kicked it to get it away from me. The dog yelped and fell onto the ground whimpering.

The men turned on me, and if it wasn't for the commander intervening, I think I would have been beaten to a pulp! All over a bloody dog!

So, the commander took the decision to shoot the dog. Seemingly, I had broken its leg. As the pitiful creature looked up at Adrik, (who had developed a fondness for it), with pleading eyes, crack! The rifle of the commander joined the other reports echoing from the gloomy forest.

Since that episode, the men had actively ignored me, and I saw them talking to each other, looking at me with suspicion and hatred in their eyes.

So now my tobacco had gone missing. No point in questioning them. The bastards all stick together. I'll get my own back. Just bide my time.

The trucks arrived. Big black Marias, slits for windows, no markings on the side. We were designated trucks, and once inside sat on metal benches as we bumped and jolted along the country lanes of Katyn.

It seemed only a few minutes later that we turned into the forest itself, the driver navigating a narrow track that appeared as though it was used for logging. After several more minutes, we stopped. From the narrow window opposite me, I could see a huge earthmover pushing the forest floor upwards as though an earthen wave. The mover finished its work, and we were let out of the trucks and ordered to ensure that our pistols were loaded.

We were lined up. Stood to attention. Pistols loaded and at the ready.

What was this?

There was a huge cavity in the forest floor where the earthmover had done its job.

The forest was silent now.

More trucks arrived this time containing the prisoners.

Polish. All officers by the look of them.

Bastards.

Can't stand the Polish, and I hate officers.

It soon became clear what our task was. And I was up for it.

I was bad-tempered and itchy this morning. I hadn't had a smoke to calm my nerves.

Thieving bastards.

Well, this might help.

The men said that I killed more than them. Looked like I enjoyed it, they said. Well, it was orders, wasn't it?

A bullet through the back of the skull. Easy. Bang. Another one for the pit. Job done.

The smell of carbide mixed with the smell of terror as some of the officers shat their pants. Pussies.

My comrades. Ha! Comrades. That's a joke. They look at me as if I come from the moon! Smiling, they said I was. How I would have loved to have turned the pistol on them!

Anyway, it's over now. Until the next convoy arrives anyway. Let the decomposition take away all the evidence! Let the forest deal with the bodies.

And so, the natural way of the earth took place underground, as the bulldozer once again returned, this time to hide the shame and embarrassment of murder.

Yes, the bodies rotted as they lay intertwined in the cold earth. But they gave no nutrition to the soil.

The oak spoke.

The oak that Pietro had passed every day as he walked into the unfamiliar forest.

The oak Sophia had rested her back on years before had now become the authoritative voice of the forest.

It spoke of seeing man destroy man.

A species killing its own species.

And said no tree, plant or animal could take any nourishment from this place, as it was a place of abomination and shame to the earth. It spoke through its roots to all of the forest, and the word spread across the land, and then to the world, that the species known as man would no longer be trusted to hold it in its care.

The forest fell silent.

And not even a weed or wildflower grew on the sites of slaughter.

A few years passed, and Pom continued to fight in the war of man. He killed many and each man that fell to his bullet meant less to him.

And then the fighting ceased.

The men that survived wearily and brokenly returned to their villages and towns; or what remained of them.

Pom's dream of going back to his village had been overtaken by something darker. He no longer wished to hunt rabbits. He wanted something more. Something that he had got a taste for back in the forest.

He got on a train bound for the city of Moscow.

He sought out the dark places. He sought out the weak; people he could control. He built a strange following. The freaks and misfits that he promised sanctuary became his puppets. And he put them on show. He dealt with those who could arrange for him to have exotic animals delivered. And then he also put them to work in his bizarre circus, cowering under his cruel whip.

He was a forbidding master to all that were under his dominion.

He befriended those in authority. He used them for his own purposes to gain more control. They in turn became cruel and perverted in his company. Officials, politicians, police and those in power became increasingly corrupt, and they helped him out wherever he went.

He made many enemies, but they rarely lived long, thus quenching the thirst he had gotten in the forest all those years ago.

And he had children. And they were all raised by Pom. And although he had all but forgotten the daughter he had abandoned, he remembered the irritation he felt over her innate sensitivity, and emotional attachments to animals.

They were all boys. And taught them the ways of cruelty.

And they were all called Pom.

As Jenny finished her story, the sound of raucous laughter could be heard from above, along with a sound of heavy footfalls. Shortly after this, a series of short taps was heard on the trap door we had come through earlier.

'The secret code!', Ami exclaimed. 'We have an arrangement with the people who run the mill that if they need to speak to us, they use a precise series of knocks on the door. I've only just remembered that, as it's never been used!'

Ami went to the stair and, releasing the door, had a short-muffled conversation. On her return, there was an air of concern etched on her face.

'There's a problem, people. I've just spoken to one of the windmill guides and he told me that a couple of odd-looking men were asking if they had seen their relatives. And then they went on to describe Jack and Jenny.

'Rum may have survived the fire'.

An air of despondency pervaded the room, as silently we all processed what this news meant.

'You must leave tonight, Jack. It seems you may have a difficult journey, but we feel that something important is going to happen and you must be there, as you are a key player now.'

Jenny looked forlorn as she relayed this news to me.

'It's OK, Jen', I said, 'I've nothing better to do. Pretty sure my boss has given up on seeing me again anyway! Where am I going?'

'Let's not talk about it now, we will brief you this evening. In the meantime, let's catch up some more!'

So, for a few hours we all put aside our fear that Rum had escaped. We spoke about anything but the looming feeling of dread that we all held inside our minds about what may come. But the minutes and hours flew too quickly past, and although we had no natural light in our underground retreat, the feeling of lateness crept into us. More coffee and tobacco were proffered before the business of my leaving was broached.

Hannah had joined in the conversations earlier, but remained reserved, and I noticed she kept sneaking surreptitious glances toward me, as she had done earlier. She spoke directly at me now, and there was authority in this old woman's voice.

'You must go to the old Yew, Jack. I don't know what you will find there but I feel it may not be good. However, we may find some answers to this new catastrophe. Remember, although you walk in the modern world, you are dealing with the ancient. It would be wise to be mindful of that. Although the distance to the Yew is not great, I think it will be a perilous journey. Unfortunately, the roads are too dangerous to use as they will be watched by our adversaries.

'Travel through the countryside as much as possible. It will be safer to walk early in the morning and in the evening. There is a pub you can use near the Yew. But be wary, Jack; although we used to use it years ago and it was safe, I'm not sure now. The landlord's name is Donald. He is a funny old goat. He'll remember me, so mention me to him; he will be surprised that I'm still breathing! You will need to head west from here; there is an ancient Yew grove that has become important to us. They were planted by local men to commemorate the victory held over the Vikings back in AD85. Even I wasn't alive then! There are some even older as well.'

Hannah was trying to inject some humour into her instructions, but her face told a different story. Although already very old, she seemed to have aged further over the past few minutes.

'There is one tree you will need to look out for, Jack. It is the oldest one. You will need to commune with it.'

'Commune with it? How on earth does that happen?'

Hannah laughed, 'Don't worry Jack, all will become clear once you get there.

'Right, well it's time to get going, the evening draws on and your feline companion is awaiting you outside!'

I had almost forgotten about '*Yellow*'!

Hannah was right. If I didn't go now, I never would. This new task seemed daunting now I knew about the corrupt power of Rum. Jenny came to me as I began to gather my small number of belongings.

'You are strong in spirit, Jack, always have been. That's why you are here! I am feeble now. I would love to come with you, but my time is soon to be over; but that's ok, I have been released from his bondage, and that is a gift worth all the treasure on earth. Be careful Jack, we want you back amongst us soon!'

'You'll get stronger, Jenny. I'll be back before you know it!'

'Jack, you know that whatever happens, you have been the best friend anyone could ever have. All the time I was in bondage, the memories of the times we spent together at the den saw me through. And now we have a legacy in Jill. Go in strength and courage Jack, remember, we are as much alive as we keep the earth alive!'

With this, Jenny left the room with Hannah.

It was the last time I ever saw her.

As the hatch opened at the top of the steps and my head poked through into the windmill's lower floor, a chill swept over me. It was cold now, but this chill penetrated my soul. Hoisting my rucksack over my shoulders and zipping up my army jacket to its maximum, I stepped out into the cold winter's night.

I had never been that proficient with a compass. I guess Hannah had realised this, so while I was sleeping the previous night, she had charged my dead phone and loaded a map onto it with directions. She had also packed a solar charger to boost the battery in the daytime. This ancient woman was a genius!

Standing beneath the huge white sails, still visible in the night, a sense of purpose unexpectedly overtook me. I was anxious about the next few days, but being with Jenny again, and meeting Jill, had empowered me. As if through osmosis, Hannah's strength and integrity had filled me with this new sense of resolution.

Someone else it seemed had the same sense of persistence, as *'Yellow'* made his presence known by making his customary growl, which if I hadn't realised it was him would have had me scuttling back to the safety of the windmill.

It soon became obvious that trying to navigate the Downs at night would be very difficult. It was so dark that the huge descending gradients of the hills were not noticeable until you went tumbling down. Very hazardous! I made, hesitatingly, for the minor roads that headed vaguely in the direction I wanted to go. Every time a car made its way down a lane, I ducked into a bush or hedge, for fear of Rum's men. Walking at night put my mind in a whole new perspective. The sounds and smells were different from the daytime.

Woodsmoke drifted into my nostrils from nearby cottages, the occupants unaware of the vagrant walking through their villages, accompanied by a strange yellow feline. Night creatures furtively scampered in and out of the hedgerows, and owls hooted from unseen trees.

I tried to focus on positive thoughts when tramping through the night, following the luminescent glow of my mobile screen. It was too easy to think of all the danger that lurked in the area, knowing that Rum was abroad.

The night air was clear and cold. As I looked up to the heavens, I realised that for once in my life I was happy! I may be in danger, and I may have lost the woman I married, and the job I thought I wanted, but I was happy!

'Are you happy, Yellow, wherever you are now, you strange, wonderful creature?!'

The thought of my old self, thinking about my current situation, talking to an oversized tabby cat and following a path to God knows where, made me chuckle with joy. My boots kept on bouncing down the dark cold lanes, stepping in puddles and car churned mud, but at this moment in time I couldn't wish to be anywhere else.

Chapter Twelve

Journey (II)

The seconds, minutes, and hours passed slowly that first night. When the magical dawn broke over the Downs, I found myself looking for a place to lay my head down, away from prying eyes. A signpost offered direction to a small town a mile or so away. I thought I would risk a visit, hoping to find a quiet café to get some sustenance.

'Yellow' had already found his spot for the day, an old broken-down barn, which he slinked off to.

'See you later, old pal', I whispered. I was sure I heard a low growl as he entered the barn.

As I walked into the fringe of the town, the beginnings of the day were starting to take shape. Paperboys and postmen were out in the early frosty streets, delivering to drawn curtain households.

The café I was looking for, as if placed for my benefit, fortuitously appeared on the corner of the approach road. The windows were misted and netted, but a dull round bulb lit a small cardboard 'Open' sign. There were a few yellow, fluorescent jacketed workmen, hunched over mugs of tea and mountainous fried breakfasts. The warm, fuggy atmosphere, enhanced by the workmen's roll ups, made me drowsy and lethargic. I ordered tea and fried egg sandwiches, rolled a cigarette from my pouch, and looked through the local newspaper that had been left on the sticky surfaced table. The usual stories by outraged locals littered the paper, bemoaning the council and other authorities. They were enhanced with staged photos of angry faced people with handmade placards, standing outside whatever municipal building was their target.

At the back of the newspaper were the classified advertisements, offering the usual services, and the usual unusual services. One advertisement caught my interest however:

The Historical Society of Sussex

We are pleased to announce all day showings of vintage local history films from 1930s onwards.

Join us in the Regal Cinema, The Thoroughfare, Friday.

I looked at the fat splashed calendar behind the counter, confirming that the day was Friday. Finishing up my breakfast, I bade farewell to the monosyllabic owner and made my way into the town. It was still only early but as I came across the old brick cinema, I saw a black suited concierge standing in the entrance welcoming crowds of people!

The interior of the cinema was furnished with red velveteen upholstery, and the walls with dimly lit art deco lamps. The curtains remained closed, but an organist was playing indiscernible melodies which were piped throughout the cinema.

I took my seat in the rear stalls and with great relief closed my eyes. I was told by the concierge that I could stay as long as I wanted to; he probably thought that I was a history nut, but my intention was to sleep through the several showings to renew my energy.

As the organist finished his repertoire, I opened my eyes briefly to take in the main show. Black and white grainy footage was playing showing rural scenes of the Downs and farm labourers smiling for the new-fangled camera. The audience appeared captivated by the vintage film of their locality; the only sounds heard were polite coughs, and the unwrapping of sweets.

I closed my eyes again. The films were mainly silent and before I knew it sleep took me to the land of dreams and visions.

I remember as a kid watching old Walt Disney cartoons. They hadn't the whizz and bang of the later animations and were tame compared to the likes of *'Road Runner'* and *'Wile E. Coyote'*, but there was a lurking menace in the monochrome Mickey Mouse in *'Steamboat Willie'* or *'The Mad Doctor'* which you couldn't quite put your finger on.

As I slouched, sleeping in the red velveteen cinema seat, the black and white projection on the screen reflecting on my eyelids, I dreamt, in monochrome. As is the way with most episodes of dreaming, recalling a timeline is difficult. What seems like an hour in a dream can be measured in seconds, (or so say the experts).

This was a dream like no other, also, one which I hope I never revisit.

I was walking through a grey woodland, the trees and ferns dripped with an early morning dew. It felt very early. Not in the day, but in the world. There were numerous birds and animals around, fluttering and scattering around me.

I was reminded of the scene in 'Bambi' where the birds and butterflies flit around Bambi's head, and the rabbits frolic around on the ground.

There was a peaceful and serene feeling to the forest, and I felt happy walking along on this day, I had never experienced so many animals around, and showing no fear to this person walking amongst them. It was a 'Zip-a-Dee-Doo-Dah' moment. I remember this wonderful scene with great clarity.

As the animals and trees seemed to embrace me into their world, flashes of colour began to appear in the forest. Grey butterflies, sitting on leaves, finding shafts of sun to warm themselves in the early morning, began to show blue and red patterns on their wings. Leaves began to adopt greens and browns, until after a few minutes in my dream I was walking in a forest of Kodachrome.

Dragonflies with iridescent greens and reds rested on my arms; a Jay landed on a branch in front of me, its mottled red breast throwing the background of green into stark contrast, its guttural call making me chuckle.

This blissful scene seemed to last for ages. I recall sitting under a spreading willow next to a clear running stream, which was full of leaping rainbow coloured fish.

It must have been about midday as the sun lulled me into a sleep within a sleep.

I awoke chilled. The sun had moved around the sky but there were no clouds covering it. I looked at the stream in front of me and the fish within it. They were still plentiful but seemed less vibrant in colour.

I looked to the near distance and the forest had taken on a dull quality. Behind me the forest was still in glorious technicolour.

Silence.

Stillness.

And then the nightmare began.

In the distance, a wall of cloud had built and was quickly moving forward towards me. The nearer it came, the colder it became.

The maelstrom was almost upon me, but I couldn't move. I continued sitting with my back to the willow, powerless in the fury that was soon to be upon me. The wall of cloud began to take form. It wasn't cloud at all, but a wall of visions. Enveloped in the churning vision were glimpses and indications of what was imminent to the earth in the very near future. It was terrible to look at.

There were images of pestilence, slaughter and famine. Huge swathes of deforestation were revealed in the maelstrom, along with unfathomable numbers of slaughtered animals, buffalo, bison and whale, to name but a few that I was able to see.

Then the wall turned into wave after wave of pollution. It rained across the oceans and countryside, tangling, trapping and suffocating every living creature in its path.

The silence was replaced abruptly with the wailing of the tortured and trapped animals. Those experimented upon, those hunted, and those bred in cruel captivity for man's hunger and greed.

After a while, behind this awful sound was a new voice. A sound of triumph and grim laughter.

The unmistakable sound and voice that I knew well.

And then a remarkable thing happened to me in my dream. The willow I was resting upon enfolded me in its limbs and trunk. And within it, a deep and sonorous voice whispered…

'M..aaa..n is co..m..ing.'

And I was enveloped and taken inside the tree, where it seemed to me in my dream that I was at one with this organism.

And.

Safe.

I remembered the words that Hannah spoke to me before I left about communing with the trees. Surely this was what she meant?

Then I awoke. The screen had the same rural images flickering on it that were showing when I fell into my dream, although this time the trees and bushes were barren and spindly like after a dose of agent orange.

I quickly gathered my belongings and left the now empty theatre.

As I strode up the same road I came in on, I tried to make sense of what had just happened. At this moment I decided not to.

The café I had stopped into that morning was still serving. Another clientele was seated at the same table the workmen had been at this morning. This time it was a group of teenagers, noisily discussing some disagreement with another friend.

I ordered a coffee and some beans on toast from the same monosyllabic server who showed vague surprise on his face at my return.

One of the teenage girls, the most vocal of them, looked in my direction as I was eating, and said, 'What's the rucksack for mate? On a hike?' This raised a laugh for some unknown reason with the others in the group.

'Yes, I'm on a pilgrimage.'

The group obviously found this response too intellectual and continued with their original conversations.

Being slightly irked at their stupidity I decided to engage them further; 'I've just been looking at some of your local history, actually.'

The most vocal replied with a sneer, 'really…ooh, how interesting!'

'It was', I replied, 'you should go too, you may learn something. It's at the old cinema down the road.'

The group then erupted into laughter. It was at this point that the monosyllabic server stepped over to my table to clear the plate.

'Son', he said, 'there ain't been a cinema or theatre here for 30 years or more.'

The air was cold and damp that late afternoon. It was the time of year when evening begins about 4pm and you feel like turning up the heating, wrapping yourself up in a blanket with a cup of tea, chocolate biscuits, and calling it a day. This, however, was not for me. The evening was getting near and I had a few miles to put in before I could rest again, hopefully at the pub Hannah had told me about.

I walked up to the junction where I had said goodbye to *'Yellow'* and looked out for the old barn he had crept into a few hours earlier. The barn appeared out of the gloom and I hesitated before ducking under some barbed wire, prolific in the English countryside, into the field where the barn was standing in the murky light.

I felt lucky that I had not encountered Rum and his cohorts since my new journey had begun, but the familiar ominous feeling of dread was creeping up on me again.

I was glad to be walking the country lanes.

A conclusion felt imminent, however this journey was eventually going to conclude.

I crept into the barn, gently calling out my feline companion's name. Powering up my mobile, I used its artificial light to scan the decrepit old shack in search of him.

The inside of the barn smelt of wet rot, and my light picked up old rusting farm machinery, left in its state of disrepair for what looked like many years. The barn had an upper loft, probably used to store hay, with an old wooden ladder leading up to it. Several rungs were missing as it led to the top. My light caught a flash of a pair of eyes, coming from the top of the hayloft. *'Yellow'!*

'Come on, old pal, do you want to come on another adventure? I may need you again!'

A low growl emerged from above, but *'Yellow'* made no move to come down. 'I guess you want me to break my leg coming up, don't you', I said, as I gingerly climbed the ladder, holding the mobile in one hand to light my way. The old ladder creaked and complained as I made my way up. As I poked my head over the top, I was greeted not with one pair of eyes but five!

I climbed over to *'Yellow'* and sat down on the damp wooden floor.

'Well, I guess that serves me right for being presuming. Who would have thought my brave friend was another girl! I guess I see a pattern here…congratulations, old girl!'.

'Yellow' was preoccupied with nursing her litter, but I was rewarded with another low growl. I stayed with her for about half an hour, fussing her kittens and stroking the exhausted cat until I thought I needed to get moving again.

'Well, you look after yourself old pal, and your lovely brood; hopefully you will be left in peace until I return'.

With a heavy heart, and tears in my eyes, I climbed back down the ladder to continue my journey. It would seem strange not having *'Yellow'* around. I was concerned about her welfare, but I was powerless to help at this time. She had been a faithful companion and I would miss her dearly.

Chapter Thirteen

The dark walk

By my reckoning, and the mobile's mapping route, I would have about five to six hours walking until I made The Yew Tree, the pub Hannah had told me about.

I would get there too late even for a pint, but I was determined to get as near as possible. At least I could get a room in the morning and sleep in a real bed before my final walk.

The first part of the walk was tedious dark country roads, dank overhanging trees dropping water on me as I made my way along them. I saw no landmarks; the only habitations were the distant farm dwellings I was accustomed to seeing along my routes.

I was doing well, however. The mobile app was showing that I was only a few miles away from the pub. It must have been around midnight.

I noticed that even the distant farmhouses were turning off their lights and no doubt Mr. and Mrs. Farmer were climbing into a feathery warm bed. I found a stile at the side of the road and made an uncomfortable seat for myself. I replenished myself with some liquid from the flask, refilled back at the windmill, rolled a cigarette from the age polished leather pouch, and with fresh determination, and the thought of a warm bed imminent, strode off once again into the darkness.

It wasn't long after this that the smell hit me. I couldn't work out immediately what it was, but something in the recess of my memory registered fear related with it.

The lane was like all the others I had tramped on over this journey, narrow and muddy, with the smell of rotting vegetation. Nature ready to turn the old year's death and decay into the new year's substance. The new smell overcame this, however; it was a rotting smell of decay, but without the promise of new life attached to it.

A boy sat in the road.

Unconcerned with danger that may come, he sat naked, and cross-legged, his torso captured in the mobile's white light. He sat pale, ulcerated and emaciated. I remembered the images shown on television when I was a teenager. Shocking images. Children with flies crawling on their despairing eyes, with bones that were barely covered by skin. I remembered in that moment, looking at the boy, the feeling I had then, of hopelessness and confusion. Why were we letting this thing happen?

And the rage in me, buried for years, that some of my classmates and their parents were scathing of the children's plight. Placing the blame not on the weather or the corruption of the tinpot regimes, but the people themselves. As if the colour of their skin and their ethnic ways were blame enough to bring on famine and disease.

But the boy in front of me was more than this. Much more. Looking into this boy's eyes, I was aware, suddenly, of all man's abominations on fellow man. All of man's abominations.

The boy's eyes were a window into hell. No words came from his puckered and deformed lips. I stood like a helpless and hopeless onlooker.

The feeling that reverberated back all those years, as I watched the television report, from hundreds of miles overseas.

I saw a Jewish child torn from her parents in a concentration camp in 1940s Germany.

I saw native Indian families shot and trampled by arrogant white soldiers, mounted on fear foamed horses, in the American West.

I saw a young girl running in a dirt road, with manmade liquid fire burning on her skin.

And I saw persecution from the beginning of man's dominion on earth: greed, vengefulness, jealousy, and hate.

Man against man, man against beast, man against nature, man against earth.

And then in this boy's eyes I saw the heart of his pain. The boy's heart was full of love. The images that he showed me in his eyes were full of hate.

The conflict in him was a terrible thing to see. His pain and suffering reached into me, as I stepped forward, and with great care, love and repulsion, lifted him from the tarmac road.

The smell of him hit my nostrils, sending me back to an earlier time when the feeling of nausea had once again overpowered my senses.

The job I had been employed to do was a simple one. There was no appeal attached to it, and in some respects, although I knew that this menial work was going to be short-lived, I was happy overall to be on the road and in the fresh air, unencumbered by too much paperwork and despondent staff grumbles, in energy sapping offices. I was employed to take samples of fresh concrete from the huge disgorging cement trucks. I carried the tools of my trade, bucket and shovel. Once obtained, the fresh mix was tamped into steel cubes in the back of a van, ready to be cured and then crushed, to ascertain the strength and durability of the mixture.

I spent much of the day chasing these spinning beasts along highways and byways, to muddy and grim building sites and major construction enterprises. But sporadically I was rewarded with a visit to the countryside. Occasionally the concrete was needed in farmyard bays, or poured gratefully along country tracks, allowing vehicles easier access in the poor weather.

I can remember this particular day clearly. Sitting in the van looking at the day's schedule and feeling with some sense of relief, that several of the day's calls would be away from urbanisation, and in the countryside.

The second visit was due to be on a farm; 'Shambles Farm.' Foolishly, I visualised in my mind the rural farms of Constable and his contemporaries - muddy duck ponds and sunken thatched roofs.

The reality of this farm was wholly different.

A concrete road led up to huge steel girdered buildings with concertina'd steel shuttered doors. An articulated lorry was reversing and bleeping up the concrete road in front of my van. It wasn't until I pulled over to the work area that I saw the trailer was carrying livestock. To this day every time I hear the reversing 'bleep' of a lorry it takes me back to that time…

Jenny and I had talked about animals at our times in the den. We were both overly sensitive to any type of cruelty, and even at 11 years old, were becoming aware of the ways of man in relation to animals. I suppose this was why I took the decision in my teens to become a vegetarian; not a popular or easy thing to do then, as the food industry was pretty much oblivious to the small but growing number of 'cranks' out there.

We often rescued small creatures when we found them. On one occasion we found a badger in a trap, in the woods that we played in. It was crying and whimpering with pain, its leg firmly held in the jaws of what looked to be a homemade trap. The creature died as we tried to release it.

It was the pleading in its eyes that caused Jenny and me to be inconsolable after our perceived failure to save the wretched creature. We told our families what had happened that day, but both of us got little sympathy from parents who were too busy, or just plain disinterested, to offer much consolation.

We found out through the playground network that one of the kid's fathers had set the trap to show his son how it was done. They were both confused and disappointed when they found the trap sprung but no animal to gloat over in its cruel steel jaws. We had buried the badger, with some ceremony, near to our den, and were vigilant in our trap hunting from that day on. The animal's eyes and whimpers never left our consciousness, however…

So, the articulated lorry lowered the ramp and began to unload its doomed live cargo, into what I quickly realised was a slaughterhouse. The pigs began their tortuous last journey into the dark. It was then that the men organising this realised that the lorry's ramp needed to be raised to allow the pigs to enter the abattoir. A pig was chosen, and then killed, and with some effort from the men pushed under the ramp which now married up to the concrete entrance bay.

The screaming from the pigs was horrific and blood curdling. I looked to the men who were now laying the fresh concrete, but they seemed oblivious to the noise and awful smell of fear, just yards away from them. I was immobile. How could this cruelty be so casually considered and accepted?

The pigs were led down the ramp from the lorry, and as they trotted past, and over their unfortunate companion, they cried.

Yes, they cried…

...the smell of this unfortunate boy had resonated with my senses taking me back to the time on *'Shambles Farm'*.

As I carried the whimpering boy to the verge, I felt at last that my sense of what it was to be human was consummated. I had been acting a part in my life, playing a role, putting on a show, mainly to see the effect it had on others. Even Jenny and Ami and those I was close to had seen this great artiste. I guess I was looking for some acceptance, and meaning in my life, which up until now had felt meaningless.

This night - cold, damp and miserable - felt real.

I felt alive and empowered, and deep inside knew exactly what needed to be done, now and in the forthcoming hours. I lay the boy to rest, leaning on a dark damp tree trunk and began to assess the situation. I took Ami's blanket from my rucksack and wrapped it around the shivering boy, but before I could think about what to do next the boy spoke.

'We need to get moving, Jack. I feel Rum is near.'

The boy was looking at me from his position on the ground, with a different type of fear.

His demeanour had altered from one of hopelessness and terror, to one of need and concern.

I was shocked to see now that his once deformed features were becoming less grotesque and more fully formed. His mouth, even in the dull evening light, was less puckered and twisted. The ulcerated face that I thought I had seen also seemed to become clearer.

'Who are you?', I said gently.'

'My name is… C…c..arn…iv..val.'

The boy hung his head for a short while. Then slowly looking up, he met my eyes and began to speak again. This time, however, the stuttering had ceased.

'My name is Carnival. That's the name Rum gave me anyway. When I was a baby, he seized me as his own. This is what he told me anyhow. He used me in his attractions. You see, when I was young Rum found out that I could contort my body and alter my outward appearance. With cunning means, he encouraged this skill of mine, and refined me, as only he knows how, to become an exhibit in his disturbing shows. Unsurprisingly, he became rich on my talents, pushing me further and further, pushing my body to breaking point.

'That was many years ago though. I escaped and travelled the world. I have tried, in vain, to find my true family. My hope is almost gone.'

Something didn't ring true in the boy's story, as he could have only been fourteen years old or so. The way he spoke was that of an older man. I had no time to question this, however, as the boy, Carnival, was probably right, Rum did indeed feel near. It was time to be moving again.

I went to pick the boy up again, but he surprised me by standing up.

'Let's go', he said.

With Carnival wrapped in the blanket, we set off. Conversation ceased as we walked the winding paths into the remnants of the night.

Hannah had told me about the grumpy landlord of The Yew Tree and had urged me to knock him up no matter what time I arrived. I was sceptical about this; my reckoning was that we would be at the pub in the early hours of the morning. Not an ideal time to wake up a grumpy old man!

Chapter Fourteen

The Yew Tree

Friends reunited

Emerging from the woodland paths, we walked into a darkened village, the hours ticking down until alarms sounded, phones lit up, and bleary eyes filled scaled kettles.

The pub stood at the northern end of the village, its sign swaying creakily and predictably in the night air.

'I've been here before.'

The boy spoke out of his silence.

'Well, let's reacquaint you, Carnival. I've got to wake the beast, and I could use some backup!'

It was 2am, the time when you are nearest death, the time when breathing slows almost to a halt, when dreams turn sinister, and nefarious characters do their deceitful business.

I knocked timidly on the door of the pub. The sound appeared to echo through the village. I imagined sleepy heads on feather pillows, momentarily twitching as the unfamiliar sound reached them.

'Knock harder', encouraged Carnival, as we waited in vain for any response from the other side of the heavy oak door.

'That's all very well', I replied, 'but I'm the one in front, and most likely to receive the wrath of Donald!'

I raised the iron hoop knocker, and at that exact moment the door creaked open with the sound of released chains from the other side. I expected an old, wizened character to greet me but was instead met with the polished barrel of a shotgun pointed at my head.

A quiet reedy voice came from behind the steel pointing at me.

'This'd better be good because my trigger finger isn't as steady as it used to be.'

As it turned out, Donald wasn't quite as fearsome as I had presumed. Once he spotted Carnival, we were welcomed with positive enthusiasm. Donald sheathed and locked his shotgun in an ancient wooden trunk and pushed it, with some huffing and puffing, into a locked cupboard at floor level.

My initial reaction to the hostelry that early morning was one of disappointment. The saloon bar of The Yew Tree was modern and cheaply furnished; the smell of the recently vacated patrons remained in the air, cheap aftershave and spilt beer assaulted the senses.

We followed the ancient landlord and sat down at the bar at his request. I had looked forward to an old English pub, with pewter tankards hanging behind the bar. Instead I was looking at pumps with the usual mass-produced lager, and menus with pictures of the food for those patrons who were either too drunk or illiterate to make a choice of meal.

Donald and Carnival were engaged in an animated discussion, both seated at a table in the corner of the saloon. As I walked over to them, Donald rose creakily from the chair.

‘It seems that I misjudged you. Jack, isn’t it? I hear from the lad here that you know Hannah, and that you are on a …. bit of a mission!

‘I guess I knew this day was coming’, (at this Donald began to chuckle quietly).

‘Hannah used to warn me about it when we were together. I used to tease her and call her crazy. I’m old and wise enough now to know that she was right. Anyway, you must be tired, and in need of food and rest. Let’s not stay in this awful room, follow me!’

Donald stood up from the chair and we followed him to a door marked:

Kitchen

Staff Only!

He pushed the door open, and with a glint in his eye exclaimed, ‘Welcome to the real Yew Tree!’

It wasn’t a kitchen at all but the pub I had imagined it should really have been. The floor was planked, embossed with spilt beer and worn to a sheen with years of thirsty, booted feet.

Oak beamed and welcoming, the room was, to my tired eyes anyhow, multi-faceted.

The hearth still glowed with embers from the past evening.

The bar had an impressive wall of whiskeys, and just two pumps, both unmarked.

'I'll pull you a couple of pints and get you some food; there's some homemade pies in the cellar. Chuck a couple of logs on the fire boys, keep yourself warm. Carnival, I've drawn you a bath; Jack can wait until tomorrow, but you can't. Follow me!'

The beer was warm and delicious, the pies even better, but it had been a long day and the food and alcohol quickly took their effect.

When Carnival returned, we barely managed to talk as we were so weary. Donald came back to the room and, gauging our weariness, led us towards another door, this time behind the bar.

He reached up to a very fine looking 50-year-old bottle of single malt.

Grasping the neck of the bottle he pulled it towards him, and the door creaked open to one side, the impressive display of whiskies slowly moving outwards to reveal yet another room.

'I'll tell you about this another time boys, now get some sleep!'

The room we were led to was small and low, but there were two old sofas and lots of scattered cushions. It wasn't long before we were laying down, both with the blanket covering our dog-tired bodies.

'I'm glad we met today, Jack. I'm afraid I'm very tired now, but tomorrow I'll feel refreshed and you can tell me your story.'

'I'm glad we met too, Carnival. Let's sleep now, before I raid Donald's whisky collection!'

As my eyes closed, images blurred in my mind, from old cinema footage, to scarred and ulcerated boys, laying in darkened rural lanes. The blanket given to me, what seemed like an age ago, was drawn up to my chin. The smell of woodland, woodsmoke and the outdoors interwoven in its weave, filled my senses, leaving me feeling secure and contented.

Mirror, mirror

Redheads brought out the worst in him.

The scratching and scrabbling from the closed desk lid was drowned out by the noise of the classroom, as the boys shifted on their chairs, scratched fountain pens on paper, belched and farted.

Rum, although he was known then as Peter, smiled to himself. It had been a good day.

The mouse had been given to him by God, although he didn't believe in God. Not the one they were forced to sing about in the dark wooden assembly hall at school anyway. That God sounded like a real drag. All that talk about sin, repenting and charity. That was not Peter's thing at all. He didn't mind some of the Bible stories. There was some bloodlust in them; he especially liked the story of when Abraham was going to sacrifice his son. Shame a do-gooding angel ruined it.

After playing with the mouse for a while, the cat had left its disorientated plaything on the doorstep of Peter's house. When he grudgingly closed the front door to leave for school, the gift had been sitting there, dazed, waiting for him. Now the creature was in his desk. Fully recovered, it was desperate for escape. Unfortunately for the mouse, Peter had other plans.

Many of the boys in Peter's class had hobbies. Stamp collecting, model making, sports; all the usual things that were more popular then, before the blue screen took over children's lives. Peter had a dark mind. Classmates avoided him; there was a bad air around him. He also had the ability to be cruel and bullying, way beyond the usual rough and tumble of school life. He had a sort of mentor, however. An ally if you like.

Mr. Finch was young then, he was in his teaching prime. Well respected amongst his peers, he managed to be able to control the children whom other teachers had given up with.

Those teachers without Finch's control of the children, turned away from bad behaviour, and slunk into the staff rooms to comfort themselves with tobacco and strong tea.

Mr. Finch had a lot in common with Peter. They were both sadists, and without vocalising this trait, they both saw in each other a shared love of inflicting pain. Peter hadn't reached the sexual fascinations that his teacher had, but in a few years that side of his personality would surely evolve.

Peter was content at this time of his life to hurt and torture those that were weaker than himself. Animals were his forte.

Today was different somehow. Mr. Finch, normally tolerant of Peter, had looked sternly at him when he was distracted with his new plaything. Peter carefully opened his desk and pushed his arm into it, feeling around for the miserable creature. He closed his fist around the warm body and began to squeeze. The doomed mouse was rightly terrified, and a squirt of warm urine erupted from the creature over the boy's hand.

'Son of a bitch!', Peter exploded. He pulled his hand from the desk, the creature followed, and scurried into the tangle of chairs and desks of the classroom.

The small number of girls in the class screamed with cartoon horror, as the mouse scurried around the room searching for refuge.

Mr. Finch walked with purpose to Peter's desk and, with a contented smile, lifted the boy from his seat by his ear.

'Well lad, it looks as though you want to entertain your classmates?

'Let's see what we can do to make them happy, shall we?'

Mr. Finch, even from the beginning of his career, had an eclectic array of torturous instruments to use on the boys and girls in his 'care'.

Dragging the boy by his reddening ear, Mr. Finch walked to the rear of the classroom and, with his free hand, pulled open a cupboard door. With a well-rehearsed, deft manoeuvre, he threw the boy, (by the ear!), into the space, slamming the door closed behind him.

'Let's see how your classmate gets on in there, shall we!'

Mr. Finch's face was puce, and his voice trembled, most likely in anticipation, as he retrieved a large padlock to secure the door, and hamper Peter's escape. The cupboard was of a size that could hold the usual paraphernalia of housekeeping; there were brooms, brushes, and large containers of unmarked liquids.

Peter had not been in this room before.

All the children were scared of Mr. Finch's instruments of torture, but somehow a beating with Mrs. Polly, (the name Finch gave to a particularly nasty cane), or a jolt from the 'hair stander', (an invention by Finch that was operated by a 'volunteer' pupil turning a handle on a generator, to produce an electric current that was conducted by cables to whatever part of the poor victim's body Mr. Finch chose), seemed to pale into insignificance to this small dimly lit room.

Peter had pretty much tasted all of Finch's torturous delights. Most had left him cowed and bruised, but never repentant. His encounter with the 'hair stander' had affected him the most. The pupil who 'volunteered' to turn the generating handle was that red headed bitch Janet. (When he confronted her on her way home from school she cried like a baby, "boo boohoo!"; he gave her good reason to cry after that).

Janet turned the handle, encouraged by Finch. To the delight of the class, Peter's hair did indeed rise toward the ceiling; his ears became pink and sore, and as the battery clips holding the cables bit into them, he cried inwardly, as the electrical current surged through his pre-pubescent body.

Several children had been put in the room in the past. They had all come out, somehow 'changed.' The boisterous lad had become sullen and withdrawn, stuttering in speech and losing control of bodily functions, much to the delight of his fellow classmates.

Janet, the vivacious red head who had turned the crank on the 'hair stander,' returned from her visit in the room with lank hair and bitten nails. Boys never flirted with her since the visit, she became lonely and isolated, a shadow of her previous self. (She committed suicide when 24, in the back of her father's car, the exhaust pumping its poison into the window with a rigged-up hosepipe. Nobody knew why she did this, though fellow pupils who heard the news surmised the reason, remembering her visit to the room and her behaviour afterwards. The truth was her guilt over the enforced cruelty to Peter years before).

Peter surveyed the room, lit by a yellowed bulb, hanging from a frayed, brown cabled cord. The room was unremarkable. Peter began to question the fear he had shown, and seen in others, when put into this room. The one common factor was that it was never discussed. No one who had come out of the room ever spoke of it.

Ever.

Peter began to think that this time in the room could be easy. A way out of the endless multiplication tables and stories from Mr. Finch's time in the army. Yes, he could get comfortable and close his eyes, have a nice nap…

Peter sat on the linoleum floor and made himself as comfortable as he could.

Before his eyes closed, (to the faint sound of Finch's multiplication tables mantra), Peter caught sight of something shiny on the floor, partially hidden by a moulding cloth.

Peter pulled out a small hand mirror. It was oval and had an ornate but chipped ceramic handle and frame. The silver had corroded on the edges of its surface, and rust had eaten some of the looking glass, making it difficult to view. Peter thought it had probably been left by the cleaner, who was often seen scurrying around when the bell rang at the end of the day. A crow like woman, who never met your eye, and never spoke to the children, she was always seen with huge globs of badly applied make up. This mirror would account for her lack of precision, he supposed.

Peter rarely looked in a mirror. No real curiosity about his body had entered his life as yet. No vanity about his hair, the green that covered his teeth, or concern about the spots that were beginning to appear on his greasy skin.

He was mesmerised. Never having looked much at his face before, he was pleased to note that he had strong features, and thick hair. The trouble began when he looked into his own eyes.

He began to feel queasy and found that he had trouble looking away from the glass. He tried to put the mirror down but found that his arm would not respond to its instruction.

The mirror began to mist and haze, as if a fog was descending over it. Peter was scared, but also intrigued by this new course of events.

Through the mist, Peter saw his life as it was….

seven times seven is forty-nine......

The dreariness of school, and the unhappiness and mistreatment in his home life. He was drawn to the boy he was viewing on the silvered glass. He was struck deeply by the unfairness of his life. The mirror exaggerated his mistreatment, fuelling Peter's anger toward the adults and children that he perceived kept him in captivity.

He saw no relief as the mirror showed him how his life continued its current direction. He saw a bigger version of himself. Lonely and poor, sitting in workers' cafés, eating greasy, repulsive food.

Peter's anger grew and grew as he viewed the images on the glass.

...nine times eight is seventy-two...

He wanted to smash it on the floor and grind the glass with his heel. But he was paralysed.

Then the images changed.

Peter saw himself moving onward in his life, growing as a man, becoming confident and sure of himself. But the prospect was changed.

Peter saw his oppressors crushed. He saw the cruelty that had so often been handed out to him, turned onto those that he detested.

And Peter became the oppressor.

He saw himself as rich. He saw himself as successful.

And he saw himself as cruel.

He saw people feared him, obeyed him, and worked for him. Peter saw his own name in lights…but this name slowly changed…

...ten times twelve is one hundred and twenty...

The letters rearranged and changed…

T..O..B..I..A..S..P..O..N..T..I..U..S..R..U..M

Tobias Pontius Rum.

His name now. In lights.

T.P Rum.

RUM.

From now on he will call himself Rum.

...twelve times eight is...

...twelve times eight is....ninety four sir?

NO! IMBECILE!

Peter heard Finch scream at the poor child who got the sum wrong, and imagined the cane, flashing down on the quaking child's knuckles.

Peter, no, Rum, smiled.

Peter was released when the last bell of the day rang.

Finch released the padlock and reached to haul Peter out by the ear.

Peter looked at Finch with a new expression, then said, 'No sir, call me Rum now', and he grinned at his tormentor.

Finch's colour drained from his face, and he stumbled back. He saw something behind Peter's eyes that unsettled him. It was the last time Finch ever punished Peter. The other children avoided him even more than before but so did Mr. Finch, as far as his teaching duties allowed him to. But each and every one of them called him by his new name.

Rum. Redheads brought the worst out in him.

Chapter Fifteen

Back to roots

Donald stood in the doorway, with two steaming coffee cups in his hand, and a large blade protruding from his stomach.

As the blood began to spread across his country check shirt, the mugs clattered to the ground, shortly followed by the landlord, slumping to the stone floor. Behind him stood a grinning Rum.

'Morning, boys!

Rum drew the sword from the ill-fated landlord's back and grinned with malice at us.

I was paralysed momentarily by the gruesome scenario but was jolted back to the present by Carnival's voice.

'Jack, quick! Follow me…. hurry!'

Looking behind me, I saw Carnival's legs disappearing into a small doorway at the rear of the room. Without hesitation, I threw myself towards the opening and followed the boy's retreating figure.

'Close the door behind you, Jack, there's a bolt on the inside. Slide it across, quickly!'

Fumbling in the dim light, I had just slid the bolt home before the door…*Thwump!*...the door bowed inwards from the force of Rum's weight. *Thwump!*...again the door held as we ran deeper into the tunnel. There were fairy lights strung along the walls of the brick arched tunnel, giving pale direction as we ran.

'Jack, we need to be careful now, the tunnel gets narrower and low.'

And it did, the brick lining changing into bare earth. The string of lights remained but, as we moved forward, roots began to appear from the ceiling.

The hammering had ceased from behind us. This was worrying; perhaps Rum had broken through! As I ran, the unnerving feeling that I would be grabbed from behind grew stronger. I ran headlong into Carnival and we ended up in a pile of arms and legs.

'Where are we, Carnival? Why have we stopped?'

'Luckily, I remembered this escape route from the last time I was here', Carnival said. 'I bet poor old Donald put us in that room on purpose, just in case of a situation like this. I suppose he didn't bargain on being killed in the process.'

'Well, fuck, Rum scared the shit out of me! Good job we were up and dressed. Poor old Donald, I was really warming to him as well. I guess we're not in Kansas anymore, Carnival. What's next, then? I haven't a clue where to go from here, and there's a maniac with a bloody great sword right on our tail.'

'You're right Jack, let's get moving! Here's your rucksack; I grabbed it on the way, thought it might be important!'

'Carnival, you are a diamond, as we say back where I come from!'

Carnival got up as far as the earthen ceiling would allow him to.

'We are travelling to the place you wanted to get to, Jack, the old Yew tree. The pub was named after it, although not many know about the tunnel. This passage is as old as the tree. I haven't been here for a while, but we can climb up and out when we get near the tree. Come on, let's go!'

So, with the difficulty of shouldering the rucksack and hunching down as to avoid the ceiling, we began moving again. The constant, nagging feeling of pursuit was never far from my mind. We made our way slowly along the still lit passage. Insects and earth dropped from the ceiling onto us, as we brushed the undisturbed construction. After a while, the root system above began to hamper our passage and I began to become fearful of our escape route. It was then I heard the awful sound.

A distant but recognisable voice.

'Oh Jack...Jacky boy, I'm here...Rum's right here at your service, Jacky boy...

'...come here you faggots; I have a sword that's not yet satisfied!'

Rum's voice had an immediate effect on Carnival; he dropped to his knees and began to whimper like the child on the road I had picked up only hours earlier.

'We are done for Jack, he's on us', Carnival said, and from the sound of wheezing and cursing not far behind me, I feared him right.

'Come on Carnival, we can't stop now! How far until we can climb up, can you remember?'

'It can't be much further Jack, but these roots are getting in our way now. The tree has grown since I last came, and the system is much bigger than before.'

With some encouragement, I persuaded Carnival to start moving again. We ducked and crawled through the roots, making slow and anxious progress.

The sound of cursing got nearer every second until Carnival stopped and, looking behind him, said in a tremulous voice, 'No further now Jack, the roots block the tunnel. We're trapped!'

I pushed my hand down into the rucksack, feeling for the sheathed knife Ami had given me.

'Looking for something, Jacky boy? Something a bit smaller than this, I'll wager!'

Rum was only a few feet away. The sword that Donald had tasted was pointing at me, along with Rum's hideous grin. He lurched forward and thrust the blade towards me. As I was crouched down, my face was the nearest point of contact for the cold steel. I was powerless and paralysed with fear.

The blade rushed to meet me. I closed my eyes. I waited to feel the pain…

…there was none.

I briefly thought that the sharpness of the blade had tricked my senses. I fearfully opened my eyes.

Rum was in the same posture as he had been a few seconds earlier. The sword was still in his hand, and it was still pointing at me. But there was something different. In the poor light, I could just make out that he had become entangled in the roots. No, not entangled. Held.

'My God, Jack, it's true!'

Carnival was leaning over me and started to laugh.

'The old prophesies were right; the trees, they save us!'

As we watched Rum's futile struggle, the roots began to weave, almost sensually, around his body until he was totally helpless. One root had made its way into his mouth, another into his nostrils and, slowly but surely, Rum's body began to jerk and heave, as he was robbed of air. Before he died, his baleful eyes bored into mine with such hatred that, even years later, I would wake from a subterranean nightmare, and, despite the coldest of nights, find my blankets drenched in fevered sweat.

I looked at the man that had been part of my life for too many years. An ordinary, but extraordinary, man. A man of nightmare and cruelty. Even in my relief at seeing the end of my tormentor, a sadness washed over me. I supposed it was like those that have been held hostage for years, becoming perversely attached to their captors.

I reached through the roots, closed the eyes which had been so full of malice, and watched as the roots began the grisly task of squeezing life from the body, as that was what they would surely do.

As the roots closed over Rum, they had also opened a route for us and, with disbelief at what had just happened, Carnival and I made our way along the passage, until we reached a set of stone steps that led up towards a wooden hatch. We climbed and, with some difficulty, managed to lever the hatch open, allowing the precious light of day to pour in and wash over our exhausted faces.

The Yew was enormous and stately. We had emerged a short distance from it and, for a few moments, stood in silence in awe of our new surroundings. Then we began to laugh. It started as a chuckle but, after a few seconds, we were rolling on the ground, barely able to breathe and pounding the earth with our fists. We didn't know why we laughed so hard; relief I guess, but it felt over. Yes, it felt as though something had shifted, and it felt good. And the Yew was our canopy, looking down on our foolishness.

'Well, you two are having fun, aren't you?'

'Ami! What are you doing here?'

'Waiting for you, of course! I'm taking you back to the mill to get cleaned up and have a good meal.'

Ami looked radiant; she heaved us both to our feet and hugged us until the remaining breath we had was exhausted. She pulled out her worn leather pouch and rolled us all cigarettes.

Ami had seen our weariness, so she gave us some Wintergreen to drink as we smoked. As the life began to seep back into my bones, I felt the need to describe what happened.

'Ami, can you believe we were helped by this tree?'

'I'm not too surprised, Jack. Hannah just sent me a text. She says that the system from this place is showing signs of communication again. I think you may have helped that. It is rare for a male to help with protecting. This Yew seems to have recognised the great part you have played in getting rid of one of its biggest enemies. You lured him to his death!'

'There is some bad news I'm afraid, Ami. Donald is dead. Rum ran him through with a bloody great sword. I don't think the police will find much of the defendant left; this wonderful tree here seems to have devoured him.'

‘Don’t worry too much Jack, I found Donald shortly after you left and called the police. They have already caught Rum’s counterpart, a very strange chap with a bowler hat. They had been on his trail for some time. Let him sort it out with the police, they have my name and details so I’m sure they will be in touch.

‘Fortunately, and brilliantly, Donald must have had a premonition about this; he wrote in his diary about all the events surrounding the Yew over the years. He added the last few lines last night, about how honoured he was to offer you both hospitality, but also how anxious he was about the dark characters hanging around in recent days. Wonderful man. Hannah will be very upset; I think they had a thing back in the day! Donald had expressed a wish to be cremated on his death, and his ashes to be spread under this tree. Quite fitting, don’t you think?

‘But I’m afraid I also have some bad news, Jack. Jenny died a day after you left. She died quietly with Jill and I by her side. She has asked that her ashes be scattered in the ‘Den.’ She said that although she was abducted from there, she also spent the happiest of her days there with you and the gang.’

I stood in shock but surprisingly also felt a small degree of relief. After all Jenny had been through, she now had some peace. My grief felt enormous, and the feelings that I had carried for so many years began to return, but this time there was a subtle, sweeter edge to them, knowing that in her death had come some resolution.

The boy spoke quietly.

'I would have liked to have met her again before she died, but I guess she is at peace now. I'm glad we met though. She was special, wasn't she?'

I glanced at Carnival. He stood with tears about to tumble down his face.

'You knew her?', I said.

'Yes, we were both in Rum's circus at the same time once. We were good friends. I miss her, she was very kind to me.'

Ami hugged Carnival and, after she dabbed his tears, we made our way back to the car, and took the short drive back to Jack and Jill.

'This has been your journey, Jack; I don't think it's over, but it needed a man sympathetic to our cause to 'show' the earth, and in particular, this piece of earth, that there is some goodness in humanity.

'That has been important.'

Epilogue

Jill and Ami had been somewhat elusive about returning with me to scatter Jenny's ashes at the *'Den';* they said they needed to stay with Hannah. I didn't believe them. These women were powerful, and I heard fleeting whispers of new plans and dangers to be dealt with. Their task would continue, with or without me.

Ami had offered me a stay at *'Green'*. It was tempting, and I thought I may take her up on the offer, but my old van seemed eager to hit the road again.

When I returned to the *'Den'*, it looked less important, somehow feebler than I remembered it from decades ago. There wasn't any sign of our imprint on it after all the years that had passed.

The tree where we had hung the swing had grown, its branches now barren from the winter winds that hustled through the woods, making me shiver and longing to be back; back where, I didn't know yet. Somewhere warmer for a while. Spain, perhaps? Just for a while, just to get my head straight after the past few months. Carnival coughed, deep and phlegmy, next to me. Yes, Spain. Do the boy good, for a while at least.

There had been some activity here. It was a place for children to play and imagine. Also, a place to plan, grow up, and stay young. There were crisp packets and empty bottles left, also the remains of a fire. Probably where we used to light ours.

'Come on Carnival, let's get this done, then we can find a nice pub to warm ourselves and toast Jenny.'

Carnival reached into his canvas bag and pulled out the urn containing Jenny's ashes. He crouched down under the large tree, and with mounting sobbing, reached into the container and scattered the dust onto the soil.

Flutter…

I pulled out a handful of Jenny's ashes and cast them away, with memories of red hair and laughter echoing around this very spot.

Flutter...

A bush next to us seemed to have a bird caught in it. A sense of foreboding once again descended on our peace. The fluttering became more insistent and, kneeling on the wet ground, I could make out a pale wing under a holly bush next to us.

Memories of Dark Lane hit me like a hammer; my head began to pound, a pain in my temples cut me to the core and a feeling of nausea swept over me.

I reached into, and under, the bush, the holly lacerating my hand and arm. The bird struggled frantically as I gradually got my hand around its body.

I carefully drew the poor creature out of its thorny prison and brought it into the light of day. Its legs had been bound together with hair, (red of course), and its head covered with a loose-fitting plastic bag. Only its wings were free, and I could feel the birds diminishing strength through them.

Carnival carefully removed the hair from the bird's legs and lifted the bag from its head. The white bird was beautiful, but its eyes showed terror. God knows what, or who, had done this to the unfortunate creature.

The feathers of the pale bird were stained now, with the blood from the cuts I had sustained from the holly bush; the creature looked a macabre sight. I reached up and with a gentle heave launched the bird into the air. It dipped and wavered in the air for a brief spell, but quickly sensed its freedom and flew. A shooting star in a dark, foreboding sky.

Carnival handed me the plastic bag that had covered the bird's head.

Old and degenerating, the bag had held sweets, probably from the 1970s. I remembered the brand and its design well, I had consumed many of these in my youth.

Chocolate raisins.

'Come on Carnival, let's get this done and get out of here. It's not a good place now; I almost hate to leave Jenny here.'

Carnival didn't say a word. He lifted the urn, and with a few deft moves sprinkled the remaining ashes in a circle around the base of the tree.

'She'll protect it Jack. No one will cut this tree, its safe now. Jenny will keep it safe from him and others like him. They don't like her kind, Jack. They don't like us.'

He took the urn and, taking the plastic bag from me, placed it in the urn, along with the hair. Then, finding one of the bird's bloodied feathers on the ground, he also placed that in the urn. With a bound, he climbed the tree, holding the urn in his canvas bag. With an agility that astounded me, Carnival placed the urn high in the crook of a branch, climbed down and kissed the trees trunk.

'Let's go then, Jack', he said.

That is the story. It's not over, not really. Carnival stayed with me; we explored the Spanish countryside and saw some wonderful scenes. We also saw more of the cruelty that man has inflicted on the Earth.

Together we scraped by a living; Carnival used his circus upbringing to entertain in small country bars, delighting the rural folk. I found labour in the fruit orchards and vineyards. I became happy again.

Jenny, Jill and our extended family were never far from me in spirit and I knew that one day I would return to England, to help with the ongoing struggle. For now, I was content.

I sat on a Spanish hillside one warm evening, pulled out my tobacco pouch and gazed at the setting sun. The earth was, indeed, beautiful. Rum seemed a long distant nightmare. I could hear Carnival in the near distance laughing with some local children, and dogs barking at the end of the day. Birds sang as they began to roost.

From a field not far away, I heard shooting. What was being shot I didn't know. All I knew was man, in his good and in his evil, was never far from my door…

Printed in Great Britain
by Amazon